in the briar patch

BOOKS BY GEORGE GARRETT

The Reverend Ghost: Poems
King of the Mountain (short stories)
The Sleeping Gypsy and Other Poems
The Finished Man (novel)
Which Ones Are the Enemy?
In the Briar Patch (short stories)

Some of the stories in this volume have appeared earlier in *Mademoiselle, The Sewanee Review, The Virginia Quarterly Review, The Georgia Review, Extantis, The Literary Review, The Transatlantic Review, Best Articles and Stories,* and *Best Short Stories 1960.* The author is grateful to the editors of these publications for permission to include these stories in the present collection.

In the BRIAR patch

a book of stories

by GEORGE GARRETT

university of texas press · austin

LIBRARY OF CONGRESS CATALOG CARD NO. 60–14310
© 1961 BY GEORGE GARRETT
MANUFACTURED IN THE UNITED STATES OF AMERICA
BY THE PRINTING DIVISION OF THE UNIVERSITY OF TEXAS

for jim and nancy meriwether

the stories

in the briar patch

We roar all like bears, and mourn sore like doves; we look for judgment, but there is none; for salvation, but it is far off from us.

ISAIAH 59:11

Let brotherly love continue.
Be not forgetful to entertain strangers: for thereby some have entertained angels unawares.

HEBREWS 13:1–2

the test

We had worked on the helmet off and on all spring, and by June when school was about over it was finished. And we thought it was beautiful. It wasn't that much work really, but we made an occasion out of each afternoon that we spent together working on it. The three of us met in the secrecy of Bobby's garage, smoked until our heads were whirling, and talked about all the things we were going to do when we were finished. It had been just like that a few years before when the three of us tried to make a raft out of the pieces of a tumbled-down old boathouse. I wanted to float along the St. John's River all the way from Sanford to Jacksonville. Then the Mississippi. Then—who knows?—the Nile, the

3

Ganges, the Amazon. When we finally got it put together and put it in the lake to see how it would float it sank like a stone. Clearly, though, the helmet would be a useful device. My plan was to scour the lake bottoms for sunken rowboats. We'd raise them, patch, caulk, paint, and sell them. With all the money we got we'd buy a good-size yacht and cruise around the Gulf of Mexico searching for pirate treasure. Bobby was more practical from beginning to end. He was for taking it out to one of the popular swimming places—Rock Springs, Sanlando Springs, Palm Springs—and charging a quarter a head to use it for, say, fifteen minutes. By the end of the summer we wouldn't be rich, not by a long shot, but still our pants pockets ought to be bulging heavy sacks of quarters. Chris, the Greek, had another idea completely. He said he just wanted to learn how to use it and to enjoy it. He would have liked, he had to admit, to go over to Tarpon Springs where most of the Greeks in the state live and become a sponge fisherman. But he had the grocery store waiting for him to finish high school, the bright rows of labelled cans, the stalls for fresh vegetables, the meat counter, the coat of sawdust on the floor, the flies and the hanging fly-paper, the rich smells of the place all mingling together, and his father, a dark little man always smiling and rubbing his hands together and with one quick finger belling the music of his sales on the cash register.

All of us, then, were thinking of the diving helmet, not just as a means to something—money, adventure, pleasure—but as well as a means to escape from something. For instance, Bobby, the practical one, didn't need money at all. He came from the richest family in town, the banker's. After the disasters of the Depression my father thought it was the best joke in the world that *his* son should have the *banker's* son for his best friend. Whenever I'd ask permission to spend the night there or eat supper at Bobby's, he'd say: "Sure, by

4

all means. Go on over there and really enjoy yourself. We might as well get *something* back from the bank."

"Hush up, Hugh," my mother would tell him. "Bobby is his friend. He doesn't have to worry about all that."

"I'm for friendship," my father would reply. "Let friendship thrive. But I reserve the right to take the ironic view of the situation. If you please." He never quite got over the hard times and the fact that he'd lost every cent of his savings, though he managed most of the time to maintain the "ironic view." He had been in the real-estate business. Now he was a full-time inventor and spent most of his time in the study with a bottle. Bootleg whiskey then, but "the real stuff" off a boat that came by night to the coast and unloaded its cargo to dark waiting low-slung high-powered cars; these sped lightless over the rutted back country roads they knew by heart. Actual delivery was performed by a Negro washerwoman with a huge bundle of rags and bottles wrapped in a sheet and balanced on her head—which might have seemed mysterious and suspicious since nobody on our block could afford a washerwoman any more and the wives could be seen any Monday morning hanging their own clothes out on the line, but the Chief of Police lived right down the street on the same block and got his liquor the same way. Anyway there Father would sit with his bottle and his drawings and papers and plans and schemes. Some of them: an airplane, *not* a helicopter, that could fly backwards if you wanted it to, chewing gum that *really* cleaned your teeth so you didn't have to bother brushing them, a pill that turned fresh water into pure gasoline, a brand new kind of coffee made out of acorns, a new kind of bulletproof glass. The funny thing is that a few years later when the War came along the latter made him a good deal of money. The Government used some part of his patented invention for the canopies and blisters of fighting airplanes. But meanwhile my mother taught

5

school, my sister put off getting married (forever it turned out) to teach school too. And my brother dropped out of school and got a job with a shoe firm as a travelling salesman. No wonder then, when I recall it now, all my thoughts were of the Amazon River and searching for buried treasure.

With Chris, as I said, it was a different thing. His people were poor even before the Depression. His father had been an officer in the Greek Army, and when the Turks drove them out of Smyrna, he came to Florida and managed to open up a grocery store. He was a thin, dark little man with a clipped military mustache. Everyone said he had been a Greek aristocrat once. (Of course they say that about all the foreigners.) Now he and his wife and Chris, their only child, ran a grocery store. If it wasn't very prosperous, it was all his, and one day Chris would have it. Chris had to work only on Saturdays during the school year. But during vacations and the summer he had to work every day. Like lots of boys whose parents were foreigners, Chris was at once ashamed and protective of them, proud and embarassed at the same time.

Bobby had furnished the basic item, a worn-out hot-water heater. It had a square piece of glass near the top where the meter had been, and that was perfect for a faceplate. It had a hole in the top where the pipe had fitted on, and that would do fine for the air line. He also furnished a jigsaw and metal files to smooth it down with. I furnished a garden hose. Chris had a bicycle pump and some rubber insulation that they use for the windows of automobiles. That was just what we needed for rough edges that would touch the body. Between smoking and talking about what we were going to do with it we did some work on it and finished up just the week that school ended. Chris was in a big hurry because he'd have to go to work right after the last day of school. We cut the heater in half and then cut out the sides of the top

6

half so that it would fit easily over the shoulders and leave the arms free, like a sleeveless, sideless vest, with solid metal fore and aft. We filed and smoothed the jagged edges and fitted the strips of rubber insulation along the edges so it wouldn't cut. We rigged up a way to stuff one end of the garden hose into the hole on top and keep it there with a great blob of tightly wound friction tape on the inside. We stuffed the little hose of the bicycle pump inside the other end of the garden hose. I painted a skull and crossbones on the back of it. And there it was, a genuine diving helmet. It looked real.

Now the question was, what were we really going to do with it? I was for starting immediately to explore the lake bottom for rowboats.

"It's full of sunk boats."

Bobby wanted to take it out and demonstrate it to the owners of one of the swimming places.

"If we make a deal right away, we'll have it made all summer."

Chris shook his head. "That's all right for you all," he said. "You can do what you want with it all summer long. But I want to have some fun with it first."

"What kind of fun?"

"What I had in mind," he said "was doing something all three of us would always remember."

"Like what?" Bobby, the skeptic, said.

"Oh, I don't know," Chris said. "Something special, something a little bit risky maybe."

"Daring?" I perked up.

Bobby grinned in his superior knowing way and didn't say anything. He lit a cigarette like a gangster in the movies and blew a series of neat concentric smoke rings. After all he'd been smoking a lot longer than we had. Anyway they were his cigarettes.

"It's just this," Chris went on. "I know you guys have all kinds of plans for using the helmet. But I kind of thought that since we had talked about it so much and worked on it all together and all that, maybe we ought to do something special, just the three of us. We ought to make an occasion out of diving the first time, a kind of a ceremony."

"A *ceremony?*" Bobby scoffed.

I was Bobby's best friend, but I wasn't on his side now.

"We got to have a test anyway," I said. "We got to test the equipment and ourselves. They always do that."

"You can *test* it in a bathtub."

"Aw, Bobby," I said. "Let's do it right."

"Why is it so important to you, Chris?"

Chris shrugged his shoulders just like his father did. Chris talked with exactly the same accent we did and used the same words and might just as well have been born in Florida like the rest of us, except every once in a while he relaxed into some wholly alien gesture, something he did with his hands, a sudden facial expression, or that shrug.

"My people have always been great divers," he said.

That seemed to satisfy Bobby as a good enough reason.

"What did you have in mind?"

"Well, I was thinking maybe we might take a boat and the helmet out to Weikiwa. Maybe we could even get down inside that cave."

"Too dangerous."

Chris shrugged. I was delighted.

"I agree with Chris," I said. "Let's take it to Weikiwa."

"I'm against it," Bobby said, "but this is a democratic country."

We decided to go out there on Friday, the day of graduation. We weren't graduating, so we decided to skip that occasion—everybody dressed in white, long-winded speeches about the road of life, prayers made up on the spur of the

8

moment that might last for half an hour, "Pomp and Circumstance" played badly by the Cherokee High School Band, and a whole lot of people (mostly girls) crying and carrying on. Bobby not only had a Learner's License, he had his own car as well, a beat-up one, but it ran. We met at his house early that morning, shucked our white clothes in favor of something more practical, packed all the diving gear in the back seat and strapped Bobby's rowboat to the top of the car. I brought a bottle of my father's Scotch. (He'd never be able to remember whether he drank it or not.) Chris had some bread and mustard and cheese and baloney from the grocery store. It was turning out fine. We got in the car and drove ten miles out into the heart of the woods to Weikiwa Springs.

Weikiwa was once, years and years before, a fashionable swimming place. There is a ghost of a great bathhouse in the woods there, a haunted, crumbling place, a sagging pavilion, a summerhouse where the ladies could sit and watch the swimming. There's even a band shell where, I'm told, once on nice summer evenings music was played. The spring itself is a deep hole, a steep drop of ground going down to an almost perfect circle of water, an eye of bright clear sulfur water bubbling out of the mouth of an underwater cave. The spring is the source of a stream that winds away through a dense green jungle of palms and palmettos and water oaks and cypress, the trees covered with vines and the stream choked with green hyacinth plants. Farther along, up the stream a few miles are some hunting camps, and if you go by boat to one of them, you'll see huge alligators and the biggest water moccasins you ever laid eyes on. Or imagined. You might as well be in Darkest Africa; it's easy to pretend you are. Weikiwa Springs is a lonesome, beautiful, abandoned place. I thought it was a stroke of genius for Chris to suggest testing the helmet there.

9

We got as near to the edge as we could with the car, and then we unlashed the boat and struggled with it down the steep overgrown slick bank to the fringe of sandy beach around the spring. We were sweating and panting by the time we got the diving gear down there too. I produced the bottle of Scotch and opened it up.

"What'd you bring that for?" Bobby said.

"You have to break a bottle or something, don't you?"

"What does it taste like?" Chris said.

"It's not so bad," I said. "It's like cough medicine at first, but it feels warm once you get it down."

"We might need it," Chris said. "That water looks cold."

So we all took long brave swallows, made faces, grinned, and felt pretty good about the occasion. Chris made some sandwiches, and Bobby offered cigarettes. We sat on the sand and drank and smoked and ate. We started feeling good and laughing about the whole thing. Even Bobby.

"Just think," he said. "Here we are drinking whiskey, and all those kids in white suits are singing 'Onward Christian Soldiers' or 'Jesus Loves Me.'"

"What's wrong with 'Jesus Loves Me?'" Chris said. He always wore a little gold cross around his neck.

"Nothing, I guess," Bobby said. "But this is a whole lot better."

We could all agree with that.

After a while Bobby put out his cigarette in the sand and stood up.

"Well, let's get going," he said.

But who was to go first? We drew straws for it. Bobby got first, I drew second, and Chris got the last turn. He looked sad, but when Bobby offered to trade with him, he said no.

"We got to do it the way the straws fell," he said solemnly.

We loaded the gear in the boat and put on our suits and

paddled out to the middle of the spring. We looked down and you could see all the way to the bottom. The water sparkled with June sunlight. We could see the sun shining into the mouth of the cave like a beam of light coming through the window of a church.

"Okay," Bobby said. "Here we go."

He slipped over the side and winced because the water was so cold. He looked very serious. He nodded his head that he was ready and held on to the boat with both hands while we slipped the diving helmet on him. Then he made a motion with his hand to start pumping and Chris grabbed the bicycle pump and began. Bobby waved a hand at us and slowly sank down into the lucent water. Chris kept pumping and I crouched over the side and watched him descending to the bottom. When he got there he walked along slowly, heavily, on his feet like a figure in a slow-motion movie. It was beautiful to see him way down there, like a dreamed-of-thing, walking along in pure brightness. But he didn't stay down long. He moved around a while on the bottom, then he took off the helmet and swam to the surface. We hauled the helmet up by the hose while he hung on to the boat.

"You got to pump more air than that," was the first thing he said. "That bicycle pump doesn't do much good."

After we got the helmet in the boat he climbed in and sat there shivering, drying off in the sun.

"Another thing," he went on. "We did this whole thing without planning at all. We ought to have signals. And we ought to go up to the car and get the rope and use it for a life line."

We weren't about to go back to the car and get a rope before we had our turns. We did agree on some signals, though: one jerk on the hose meant to pay out more, two jerks to pump harder, three that you were ready to come up.

"How did it feel?" I said.

11

"Not so bad," he said. "You can't move around very much and the pressure hurts your ears."

"Do you think we can get in the cave?" Chris said.

"I doubt it. Not without some extra weight of some kind."

We weren't going to the car for a rope, but we didn't mind paddling back to the bank to scout around for some good-size rocks to weight us down.

Now it was my turn. I slipped into the water and had to holler it was so cold. My voice echoed in the still woods around us. They put the helmet over my head. It felt heavy and wet. The faceplate made all the world look a little watery and blurred. I took a big rock in each hand and started to sink down. I was a while getting my feet on the bottom. It was a long slow graceful fall like falling in a dream. I could hear the *squish, sqush, squish, sqush* of the bicycle pump, and the air filled up the helmet and bubbled out under my arms and shoulders. The white sand on the bottom was soft under my feet. I looked straight up and there the boat hovered above me on the surface like some kind of flying thing. The water was so clear it seemed of no more substance than the heat waves that dance on summer highways. I set down my rocks for a second and gave one jerk for them to pay out more hose, then I picked up the rocks again and started, like a creature made of lead, toward the mouth of the cave.

The water boiled out of the cave and my ears were ringing from the pressure. I fought it and managed to slip inside a bit, enough so that the mouth of the cave was behind me. Inside the cave was dark and slippery, but a flow of sun streamed past me and lit up some places with a soft glow. I could see that the cave went back a ways, and then it was too dark to tell what happened. My head was full of rushing noises. I had to keep fighting all the time to keep from being pushed right out of the cave. The air from the pump seemed very scarce and thin. I knew I couldn't get any farther, so I quit crawling and fighting and let the water wash me backwards out of the cave. When I was back on the bottom again and able to stand I signalled them to pump harder. I took a deep breath and shed the helmet and shot up to the surface. For a minute I just floated on my back and stared into the vague blue heart of the sky, dazzled by the hard light.

"How was it in there?" Chris yelled.

"Great," I said. "I got in the cave, but I didn't have enough weight to go anywhere. It was great."

"Come on," Bobby said to Chris. "Give me a hand with this helmet."

I swam to the boat and waited alongside while they hauled the helmet in.

Chris was smiling now. He had a plan. We paddled over near the entrance of the cave and threw in all the rocks we had collected. They splashed and seemed to float and turn over end over end to the bottom. He was going to have as much weight as he needed to keep him down.

"In a way I'm glad I got to be last," he said. "You guys tested it. Now I'm going to *do* something with it."

He dropped lightly over the side without splashing much or rocking the boat and held on. He had a big white smile and the gold cross around his neck glinted in the sun. For the first time I noticed how dark-skinned he was.

"I'm going straight in the cave."

"We should've brought a flashlight."

"Next time," he said. "Next time we'll bring one along."

"Be careful," Bobby said. "Don't get the hose fouled down there."

"Come on," Chris said. "Put the helmet on me."

We put it over his head, and I picked up the pump and started pumping. It was hard work and kind of tiresome. I pumped as fast as I could for him and Bobby kneeled and watched him go. He gave a jerk on the hose and Bobby paid it out.

"He's got a whole armload of rocks," Bobby said. "That's what we needed, more weight."

After that Bobby didn't say any more. There wasn't anything to see. Chris had crawled inside the cave. Every once in a while there would be a jerk and Bobby would throw in some more of the hose. Finally that's all there was to it.

"He'll have to come on back now," Bobby said.

I was sweating all over and my arms ached from pumping. I just nodded and kept on. Chris jerked on the hose again.

"We forgot to make two-way signals," Bobby said.

He peered over the side. The hose was taut. Then there were three jerks. He was coming up. We were relieved, but nothing happened. The hose slackened all right, but Chris didn't come up. Then there was a good deal of slack floating loose in the water. Bobby gave the hose a tug.

"You keep on pumping and I'll dive down and see if anything's wrong."

I was too tired even to nod by then, but I was worried about Chris and pumped as hard as I could. Bobbie dived over the side, tilting and rocking the boat.

When Bobby came back up his face was white and drawn. He held up one end of the hose to show it to me. I felt like I was going to faint.

"Damn you!" he said. "Stop pumping. It isn't doing any good."

Chris was down there somewhere with no more air. We hoped he would come up, shooting up in a stream of bubbles from inside of the cave with a great big smile and a wonderful, improbable story about all the things he had seen. We didn't even think that it was sure to mean losing the helmet. After a minute or so (so quiet we could hear the squirrels scrabbling in an oak tree up near the ruined bathhouse) we

14

knew we would have to go down and get him. We dived and dived, but even holding our breaths as long as we could stand it, we couldn't get far into the mouth of the cave. Spent, we clutched the boat and looked into each other's eyes.

"I'm going to get help," Bobby said. "Keep diving."

He swam to shore and I saw him grab up his pants and start scrambling up the bank. Just as I went down again I heard the car engine start. When I came up for air he was gone.

I kept on diving down until my lungs turned into tripe and my eyes felt like running sores. But I never could get inside the cave. When they came I was so weak they had to pull me out before they could get started trying to locate Chris. I was weak, but I remember when I got my feet on the ground I fought them to try and get back in the water again. They had to drag me to the ambulance and I was cursing them and yelling at them every step of the way.

The funeral was something else again. A terrible occasion when you didn't know whether to laugh or cry. It was at the Episcopal Church because there isn't any Greek Orthodox Church in our town. All of Chris's buddies were told to dress up in our boy-scout uniforms and act as a kind of honor guard. We still had the old-fashioned uniforms then, shorts and knee socks and the wide-brimmed, soft-crowned caps; and for high-school boys it felt pretty silly. Chris never gave a damn about the Scouts anyway, but his parents did or at least they thought he did. They even buried Chris in a Scout uniform. At least he was First-Class. Bobbie was an Eagle Scout, and I was the oldest Second-Class in the county, if not the country. We all had to file by the body in the undertaker's parlor and salute before they took it over to the church. There was old Chris with make-up on and, I swear,

15

rice powder or something to make his dark face look lighter.

The church service wasn't so bad. At least it had enough ceremony to suit Chris, lots of flowers and music and prayer read out of a book instead of made up by some windbag. It was at the grave that everything happened. Chris's mother started carrying on in the foreign way, wailing a kind of tune, crying and wringing her hands. Chris's father had on his old Greek Army uniform with a lot of medals on it. It looked strange and didn't fit too well any more. He put his arm around his wife, but he didn't seem to want her to stop wailing. Then when they lowered the coffin we all lined up and saluted and Lonnie Jones played taps on the bugle. Lonnie is the world's worst bugler (he used to drive Chris crazy at Scout Camp), and I tell you I'd rather have heard anything, even a Bronx cheer, than Lonnie Jones playing taps over Chris's grave.

After the cemetery service was finally over we all filed by the grave and threw in dirt and started to leave. I was going to ride home with my family, but before I could get to them my father saw Bobby's father in the crowd. And *that* was a scene!

"You've got a nerve!" my father yelled at him. Daddy was drunk, I could tell. "You've got your nerve to show your face here. Diving helmets! It's your money that killed that poor boy and like to have killed mine. No, no, no, it *wasn't* your money, it was our money, *my* money, you crook!"

All the time my mother and my brother Joe, the travelling salesman, were trying to get my father back to the car. He didn't give them any trouble. He let himself be led along easily enough. But still he kept twisting around his red face to shout insults at Bobby's father. Bobby's father just stood there in the sun and looked at him proudly, as if he were beneath noticing. He looked at my father as if he didn't really see or hear any of it, as if he were lost in graceful thought. He was a slim, distinguished man with white hair and one of the gentlest faces I've ever seen. He never raised his voice at anyone or got drunk in public or did anything that might possibly embarrass his family. Of course a few years later it turned out he was and had been a crook all along just like my father always said, and he shot himself. That's another story. I won't go into it except to say that even *that* gesture was frustrating to my father. He felt cheated, I guess.

"You see," he said when he heard the news that the banker had killed himself. "You see! People like that never get their just deserts. They have their cake and eat it too. God damn them all to hell!"

With all that going on at the cemetery I decided to walk home. Nobody was going to miss *me* in the excitement. And I cut across the graveyard, picking my way among the tombstones, old and new. I came over a little slope of ground and I found Bobby sitting under an oak tree smoking a cigarette. He gave me one too.

"Did you see all that?"

"Oh, I don't blame your daddy at all," he said. "I guess I'd be pretty mad myself if I was him."

"You don't feel like it was your fault, do you?"

He just shrugged. It was exactly like Chris's shrug, a real weary kind of a gesture, and for some reason it made the hair stand up on the back of my neck, and I felt a chill even though I was wringing wet with sweat in my Scout uniform.

"You don't feel *responsible,* do you?" I asked.

"Somebody's got to be responsible," he said.

"What do you mean by that? It was Chris's idea as much as it was ours. He wanted to go there and go down in the cave in the first place. It's a sad, terrible thing, but it isn't anybody's fault."

"That's the trouble with people like you, yes, like you and

17

Chris both. And your daddy and my daddy too. All you people with so much *imagination.* You have all these crazy wonderful schemes and ideas. You don't care what the risk is. And that's all right for you. But somebody has got to watch after you all the time. And when you're all finished with whatever you're doing somebody has got to come along and start to clean up the mess you leave behind. You people are like babies in this world."

That was about the longest speech I ever heard Bobby make. He sat there puffing on his cigarette with all those Eagle Scout merit badges staring me in the face and grinning at me and gave me a lecture. There was some truth in it, but it made me mad.

"Who are you, God? How does it make you feel to think like that?"

"It makes me feel old as hell," he said.

He stood up and brushed off the seat of his Scout pants and put out his cigarette. He tore it up and scattered the shreds of tobacco and wadded the paper up in a tight little ball and threw it away. (I was to learn what "field stripping" a cigarette was some years later.) He wasn't going to shame me that way. I deliberately threw mine still smoking into the grass to let it burn out of its own accord. Then, for some reason, he smiled at me and stuck out his hand to shake hands.

"Look," he said. "There's no use having an argument. Chris is dead and we can't change that. We can't ever change anything."

So I shook hands with him, and we put on our hats and started walking home.

the gun and the hat

It was Saturday afternoon and so when the dusty pickup truck came too fast down the street, heedless of street lights and stop signs, and shrieked to a trembling stop like a dog on a yanked leash in front of Estes Hardware Store, not even anywhere *near* the curb, there were plenty of people, loafers and loungers, shoppers and spenders, to look up and wonder what in the world it could be that brought Red Leland to town in such a fury. One thing you could say for Red, poor boy, he was nothing if not a careful man, an unhurried man. Hard times and bad luck teach a man patience. The weather, the years, and more than his share of tribulation had worn him, tanned and seamed his face, pursed his lips so he always looked ready to spit or kiss, and all but swallowed up the rich baritone voice you could hear

19

fully, clear and true as a fine bell, only on a Sunday morning, coming from up in the choir stall of the First Baptist Church.

He swung out of the cab, long-legged and grim, came around to the other side and literally dragged the fat boy from his seat, lifted him with one hand over a space of pure air with the boy's (his son's) feet dancing like a marionette's. The door on that side of the truck remained open, awkward on its hinges, like a broken wing. Red had three grown daughters to worry over and a sickly wife, and only one son, the fat boy, enormous for his age really, so burdened with flesh you could hardly call him a boy at all; and he surely couldn't be counted on to grow into a vigorous manhood that would ease Red's hard years on the farm. They said it was something wrong with the glands, something that couldn't be cured.

The tall man in neat and faded work clothes stepped over the curb and moved across the sidewalk, pulling the fat boy behind him, the boy crying silently, thick gleaming tears in his squinty eyes and running down a face as sad and featureless as a moon by day, streaking his cheeks with long rivulets. On the sidewalk people gave way, stepped back to make a path for them. Somehow ashamed, they turned away and wouldn't look. Inside the store fell the silence as swiftly as if someone had switched off the sound of voices with a flick of the thumb. They moved back away from the long counter and stared at the shelves along the wall. Red Leland stopped then and stood with the boy beside him, both of them limp and relaxed now, just standing there holding hands side by side at the counter waiting until Wayne Estes came to them and grinned.

"Something for you, Red?"

"I want a gun."

That stiffened them all so suddenly they might have

turned to stone on the spot. They knew, too, everyone around did, about Red's thing. It came from the Bible. Years before, young and gangling then, clutching a cheap black Bible to him like a bouquet, he used to stop them on the street and pester them about it. "The Bible say *Thou shalt not kill*," he said over and over again to anyone who wanted to or couldn't help having to stand still long enough to listen to him. "Now it don't say *what* thou shalt not kill. It just say you ain't supposed to kill, period! And what that means is everything in God's whole creation, everything living, growing, breathing, every kind of creature under the sun." He wouldn't, not in those days, hunt or fish or even eat meat. But that was when he was a young man, still a boy, before he married and before he had to go to the War. Nowdays he didn't talk about it any more. He fished the lakes in the county because he had to, ate whatever he could get and afford just like everybody else does, when he could get it for himself and his family. But still to this day he wouldn't hunt, though the truth is the hunting was good out around his farm. He wouldn't allow anyone else to hunt his land either, and some said they had actually *seen* the small brown white-tailed deer come dainty-footed, printing their neat small hooves in the soft dirt of his cleared field, to eat out of his hands. It was for sure he'd never allow a weapon of any kind in his house. Some said he wouldn't kill a snake to save his own skin.

Wayne Estes' immemorial, impersonal storekeeper's smile flickered, but retained its constancy.

"What kind of a gun would you have in mind?"

"Any kind, so long as it works and don't cost much. A cheap one."

"You want a rifle or a pistol? Or maybe a shotgun?"

Red Leland hunched forward, bowing his head to think about it, until his face nearly touched the smoky waxed finish of the counter. He shut his eyes and, freeing the boy's hand, pressed his own huge hands into the wood. It wouldn't have surprised a soul if, when he stood up tall again, the image of his two hands had remained fixed forever in the glossy wood, like prints left in soft cement. He straightened up and his arms fell loose and slack at his sides.

"A pistol will suit me just fine so long as it's cheap."

"I got a secondhand Police .38 Special here. It's pretty old and wore, and I'll let you have it for ten dollars."

"Is that the best you can do?"

"Oh, I got better pistols than that."

"I mean the cheapest."

"Afraid so."

"All right, I'll take it," Red Leland said. "Give it to me."

Wayne Estes turned around, bent his clean, white-shirted, sweaty back, and opened a drawer. It was bulging with old pistols—an Army .45, a snub-nosed Banker's Special, long-barrelled target pistols, even a little Lady's pistol, shiny and nickleplated—all with tags on them. He found the .38 and put it on the counter. Red Leland made no movement to reach for it, to touch it, to examine it, so Wayne Estes picked it up again, untied the string around the grip, and let the tag flutter away out of sight behind the counter.

"You want some shells for it?"

"Just give me a load," Red Leland said. "I ain't planning to use it but one time."

Very slowly, taking his own time about it, Wayne Estes walked the length of the aisle behind the counter, opened another drawer, rummaged there, and returned carrying a small squat box, heavy in his hand for the size of it. He counted out six of the shiny bullets and put them in a straight row next to the pistol on the counter.

"They cost thirty cents each."

"That's a lot for such little things."

22

"That's the price."

"Okay," Red said. "Load it up for me."

He broke open the barrel and placed the shells one by one in the cylinder. When all six were neatly, cleanly in place, he snapped it shut again and put the gun back on the counter. Red Leland fished deep in his pockets, and then his hand appeared clutching a soiled crumple of bills. He counted out twelve one-dollar bills and smoothed them, put them in a pile. Wayne Estes handed him the pistol, and his whole hand closed over the shape of it, loose and easy, as if he'd just picked up a rock to throw. The two men stood staring at each other, unblinking, and Wayne Estes' smile slowly waned, grew faint, vanished at last like a forlorn ghost.

"Well—?" he said finally.

"I still got twenty cents change coming."

Wayne Estes chuckled, shook his head, and tilted back for a wide-mouthed laugh.

"I'll be damn," he said. "I'll just be damn. I clean forgot about your change. How about that!"

He hit the cash register, and the little bell that tolled for all his sales, rang over the whole county's needs, desires, and sometimes luxuries, chimed liquid and clear like birdsong in the hushed room. He gave Red Leland two dimes, and then the man and the fat boy, hand in hand again, walked slowly out of the store. Just at the door the boy snatched for his freedom, failed, and started to scream as the man took up the whole weight of him, arms and legs flailing vainly like a beetle on its back, carried him to the truck, sat him on the seat, and slammed the door to.

"Well, now," Wayne Estes began, but ceased there as Red Leland loomed again in the doorway, framed now by the brilliance of the Saturday afternoon outside, his shadow spreading in a quick stain on the floor.

"Where does he live?" Red Leland said.

23

"Who? Where does who live?"

"The teacher."

"What teacher? Who are you talking about? Which one?"

"Never mind," he said. "Let it be. I'll find him all right."

This time they waited until they heard the growl of the pickup's engine and then the soprano noise of its tires as it rounded the next corner down the block much too fast before they all began to talk at once with a sudden inexplicable rising like the sound of a field of locusts at twilight.

John Pengry sat cross-legged in a bathtub of cool water reading a book. There was an old-fashioned electric fan, big, black, strutted like an early airplane, standing on the toilet and it stirred the lukewarm air around him, with each turning troubling the pages of the book. John Pengry was a small, slight man with the pinched, bony face and darkly shining eyes sometimes seen in pictures of desert fathers or the fakirs from the East, ascetics, hermits, some of them saints, those few who have been for a long time alone in some naked landscape, companioned by a cruel sun, the chill darkness, wild beasts and voices, utterly comfortless, yet strangely tempted beyond telling or believing.

He lived alone in a rambling frame house at the edge of the town. He was alone now since his mother had died and his sister Louise had left—God alone knows why, at her age—to live in New York City.

That was a strange thing. They had come straight home, just the two of them, from the funeral, and they were standing together, still dressed for it, still wearing their hats, in the living room. The light there was dusky and submarine, filtering through the drawn blinds and the green shield of potted plants on the window sills. And at that moment it was as if neither of them possessed any substance, any flesh or

24

blood or bone, as if they existed only by virtue of the vague light, as if they were floating, bodiless, amid the crowd and clutter of her furniture and her things. He felt as if the light was passing through them both like an X-ray and as if for once they were entirely composed of it, of sourceless broken light and tiny dancing dust motes. He imagined just then that if he shut his eyes and held his breath, he'd vanish, leaving the room with all its things and all the plants—so many of them, so huge and ungainly, hedging the windows —forever as it was, sealed like a tomb. It was so quiet that he fancied he could hear the plants breathing.

"You better see to getting yourself a maid," Louise said. "Someone who can keep things clean and do a little cooking for you."

"Why? If we get a maid, whatever will you find to do with yourself?"

"I won't be here any more," she said. "I'll be leaving tomorrow for New York City. Of course *you'll* want to stay."

How long she might have harbored such a curious notion, even secretly saved for it, it seemed, for she had never asked him for money, not for the trip and not once since she had gone, he could only guess. That she was in good health and working he knew from the crisp, formal letters he received from time to time, on holidays and private occasions. He replied always with long letters full of nothing but the news of the state of things in the house. There was so little for him to write her about. Whether or not she was happy now where she was, he did not know. The only thing he was certain of was that she had been right, that it was she, not he, who had been freed by that death. It had not occurred to him then or since to protest that he, too, had done his share of service and ought to be entitled to a life of his own as well.

So he simply stayed on, custodian to his mother's distant

25

trophies of an imagined (for him, anyway) past life, a random accumulation of odd things like the shells, broken or whole, the starfish, the strange growths and creatures left on a beach as a mute signature by the retreating tide. He remained in the rude country town that they (his mother, Louise, and himself) had never even belonged to or acknowledged. Though his father had been born there, he died before John Pengry had more of him to remember than the rough skin of a large face that loomed over him like a full moon, grinning, the harsh laugh, the strong warm hands in which his own child's bones felt frail and small as a bird's, and the mysterious rich odor of his breath which John Pengry was to learn years later was only the smell of strong cigars.

Forsaken by all his blood, living and dead, John Pengry remained. He hired a colored woman to come from time to time, to clean and dust, to take the white covers off the furniture in unused rooms, to throw open windows and let in light and air enough to sustain the house until her next visit. He watered the plants, which grew enormous and unkempt, a jungle of them now. He wound and tended the grandfather's clock—his great-grandfather's in fact—and he kept the solemn, familiar pictures of his ancestors in place, straight on the wall. Soon the cleaning woman was lost too. When, by an accumulation of chips and cracks, by the misplacing and rearranging of objects, it was apparent that she could not humanly perform her duties without a careless disinterest, he took over all the functions of maintaining the house, at least the interior. He didn't care how it looked from the outside. From then on he lived completely alone.

Of course he could be seen twice a day during the school year coming and going from the Seminole Grammar School, where he was the teacher of the fourth-grade boys, neat and clean, but clearly eccentric, dressed in an old-fashioned way with a high shining starched-stiff collar and, too, just a little absurd, with one of his father's suits luffing around his skinny frame like a sail in the wind. And on Sunday mornings he went to Early Service at the Episcopal Chapel (for this was not an *Episcopal* town) taking his place always in the same back pew, to kneel, to rise, to sing with the others, and to walk forward, like a man in a dream, to partake of the Holy Communion.

John Pengry was not insulted, injured, or offended by anything that happened out there, beyond the walls and windows of the house. He taught, well enough, a whole generation of interchangeable little boys, aware of them chiefly as faces which shone and wavered in front of him like a field of wild flowers in the wind. Annually he introduced them to the mysteries of long division and to some of the secret things of this earth—how coal comes to be, and where lies in dark splendor the Caspian Sea. He dealt out to them the necessary, conventional, two-dimensional figures of history like a hand of cards. He encouraged them in penmanship and led them in singing. Teaching to earn a living, to maintain himself and the house, troubled him very little. Afterwards it always seemed that he had only dreamed it. He thought of it as wholly unreal. He was a ghost teaching ghosts.

Here in this house, where he sat in the tub enduring the hot still Saturday afternoon, was as much of reality as he could bear. And it was with real ghosts, the ghosts of his mother, his father, and now more and more especially of his great-grandfather, that he wrestled. It was with them that he argued or conversed. They were his only friends and enemies.

He stood up, tossing the book aside, and he took a towel off the hook and dried himself. He put on his mother's silk dressing gown, a fragile thing of pale pink, furred at the neck and the cuffs, and he walked out of the bathroom leaving the tub still filled with cool water over which the fan, still running, cast a regular, rippling breeze. In the living room there was a round miniature of his great-grandfather done in pastels. It showed, crudely, a face like his own, the same nose, the same pinched cheeks and high cheekbones, thin sandy hair, the same dark shining eyes. But for the careful pointed beard, it might as well have been a portrait of himself. Except for the difference, the enormous difference. John Pengry stood looking at it for a while, then he went across the living room to the yellow china humidor where he kept his cigars. He took one of them, twirled it in his palm, bit off the end, and lit it with a kitchen match, deeply inhaling.

The thing on his mind was his great-grandfather's hat. It was not that his great-grandfather had been a man of great success as a planter, so successful, indeed, that a portion of his riches somehow survived the War and the Reconstruction, endured even the careless bravado of his grandfather and the reckless spending of his mother's older brothers, so that now a small part of that original rested in the bank untouched; for he would no more take it or draw from it than he would sell the house and auction its contents. It was not exactly, either, that his great-grandfather had been modestly celebrated as a man of action, one of those around whom legends and stories circle like a magic ring of doves; nor that all of John Pengry's life his great-grandfather, in reality a small man like himself, had towered so tall over all of them, casting a huge shadow like some smiling giant in a children's tale. What troubled John Pengry was his great-grandfather's hat. And, too, the manner of his death, not the facts, but the manner of it. The hat, one that rested, sacrosanct in a glass case in the living room, one that he had been as a child forbidden to touch, had been the cause of his death. It was a gray, wide-brimmed Confederate officer's hat, but it had been greatly altered by women and it bore a burst of ribbons and tassels (they were faded now, pinned around the crown like a dim rainbow); and it was plumed with a high, foolish shock of feathers, the feathers, he had been told, of rare, exotic birds. That plume, once bright, still stood up high and straight. In the crown of the hat there was a hole the size of a quarter where the bullet that had killed him entered. Inside it still had dark stains from his blood. The hat had come back to the family after he had fallen, had been brushed and cared for and kept safe under glass. But, John Pengry wondered, what kind of abandon or buffoonery had possessed the man to wear a hat like that in a war? How had he lived as long as he did wearing it? And what, after all, did it mean, that kind of rashness, except that he must have known that the hat would remain long after his bones were powder, to be attended to, to trouble and perplex his seed like a kind of curse or spell until the last of them were gone from the light to dust too?

John Pengry, puffing on his cigar, standing there in his mother's pink silk dressing gown, carefully opened for the first time in his life the forbidden case and removed the hat. He placed it on his head and, catching sight of his image in a mirror, cocked his head this way and that, like a child at a costume party.

Red Leland stopped the pickup truck in front of a sprawling, sagging frame house, so weathered it seemed paintless, set back a way from the street on a lawn as shaggy and wild as a bearskin. Azalias along the edge of the front porch grew in a crazy tangle of green, and there was a large swing on the porch, hanging by only one of its chains, lopsided. He climbed out of the cab and walked part way up the lawn. The fat boy sat in the cab looking straight ahead. Red

Leland began to call softly. He called in a steady, singing monotone, and getting no answer, seeing no sign of anyone, he moved closer and called louder. After a little while the front door opened a crack and around it appeared a thin face, intent and curious like a squirrel's, and above the face perched the most amazing hat that Red Leland had ever seen.

"Come on out. I want to talk to you," he said.

"Oh I can't," the face replied. "I'm not dressed to come outside."

"Come outside now or I'm coming in."

"In that case—"

John Pengry walked out the door and stood at the edge of his porch looking at the tall, wild-eyed country man. The tall man, blinking, looked back at him, studied him for a moment, then he walked briskly back to the parked pickup truck.

"Is *that* the man?" he said. "Are you sure that's the man?"

A boy looked at John Pengry and nodded. The tall man came back toward the house. John Pengry watched all this and wondered.

"I'm going to kill you," the man said.

Dazed by this, John Pengry merely nodded.

"You know why? You know why, don't you?"

"I don't believe I've ever laid eyes on you before," John Pengry said at last. "I'm afraid I don't know you."

The tall man whirled and ran back to the truck this time. He snatched the fat little boy from his seat and ran back, dragging him along behind at arm's length.

"You know the *boy*, don't you? You recognize *him*?"

"No, I'm sorry, but I'm afraid I don't. Little boys all look alike to me."

30

"*You teach him. He's my son.*"

"Oh, I see."

"Well now you understand why I'm here."

"I'm trying to, but really—"

The tall man seized the boy and pushed him forward to the edge of the porch. He seemed to be a very fat little boy.

"Look at him."

"I'm sorry," John Pengry said. "I seem to know them when I'm in class, at the schoolhouse. I can remember them there. But here, out of the right context, so to speak—"

"You mean you don't even *recognize* him?"

"Please be patient with me," John Pengry said. "I'm doing the best I can."

"You made a joke about my boy," the tall man shouted. "You made some kind of a joke about him in front of the whole class. He come home so choked up and ashamed he couldn't even talk. I've taken just about enough in this world. I've followed the paths of righteousness as near as I could, and the Lord has chosen me for my share of tribulation. But the Lord couldn't have meant for my seed, my own flesh and blood to be laughed at. He give me affliction. He give me troubles. He give me this little fat boy for my only son. But this last, this making jokes, is more than a man can bear."

"I'm sorry," John Pengry said again. "I don't recall doing such a thing. But if I said or did anything foolish or wrong, you'll have to forgive me."

"You don't even *recall* it?"

The tall man raised the pistol that he had been carrying in his right hand and pointed it. It was curious, John Pengry thought, that he felt so lightheaded that he wasn't even afraid.

"I say I apologize for anything. I apologize for everything I've done and left undone," he said. "It *could* have happened. Sometimes I'm not really responsible."

31

"Take off that hat."

John Pengry shook his head, feeling the weight of the feathers.

"Take off that hat. I've stood for more than enough from you."

"Go ahead and shoot if you want to, but I won't take off this hat."

"Great God Almighty!" the tall man yelled. "I ask you for a sacrificial lamb and you send me a lunatic."

Then the tears began streaming down his face. He closed his eyes and pointed the gun straight into the blue heart of the sky and fired it six times, wincing at each shattering report. When he had finished firing, he threw the gun away. It soared brightly into the maze of azalias and disappeared.

"I might have known I wouldn't do it when the time came," he said. "The hand of the Lord is on me still."

He took up the little fat boy in his arms like a baby and carried him to the pickup truck. He didn't look back. He climbed in the truck and drove away.

John Pengry locked the front door behind him. He tiptoed into the living room and peered through the camouflage of plants, holding the venetian blind aside, watching the pickup truck dwindle away down the long dirt road to the country, a furious roll of dust pursuing it. He thought he'd better wait until after dark to go out and hunt for the gun. It certainly was curious. He would mention it the next time he wrote a letter to Louise. In the meantime he might just as well climb back in the tub and cool off. In any event he would not put the hat back in its glass case. He'd want to have it handy in case those two came back.

After his father had stopped crying and slowed down a little, the boy reached over and patted him on the leg with his small soft white hand.

32

"Never mind, Daddy," he said. "It don't make no difference to me."

And then for some reason his father threw back his head
and laughed.

"Sure, boy," he said. "By God it was worth the price of the
gun to see a sight like that. What a sight to behold! Come
on, let's us go on home."

the last of
the spanish blood

That was the summer my cousin Harry came to live with us. We weren't going anywhere that summer because the war was on. Harry's father had to have a serious operation and go all the way to Baltimore to have it. He would be in the hospital a long time. Aunt Jean would have to go and take a room near the hospital to be with him.

So Harry came to stay with us.

Harry was just my age, but I didn't know him at all. They seldom came to any of the family gatherings. Except, of course, the funerals. Everybody, cousins and uncles and aunts and pets, people you never heard of, showed up for funerals. A good-size family funeral was pure delight for the children, I remember. We ran free underfoot. There would be too many grownups around, and they'd be too stiff and sad and soft-footed to bother about scolding children. The only thing you had to do was to behave in the church. The rest of the time, the days before and after, was all yours. And I vaguely remember Harry from those times, dark, about my size, shabby, because his branch of the family was poor, quick-tempered, apt to throw a tantrum, but shy, too, as a wild animal is shy. Not timid, that is. Just not tame. I had a strange idea about him even then, the kind of notion a child will pick up and hold like a coin in the palm and flip, heads or tails, just for the fun of it. As I say, Harry and I were about the same age and size, but he had dark hair and I was redheaded; and in temperament and interests we were from the beginning just the opposite. So I used to think (if you can call the flow, the torment and joy, the visionary dance of a child's mind *thinking*) that we were really the same person somehow and that when I looked at him I was really looking at myself, changed and different, strange and wonderful, the way your own face and body comes back to you as a stranger from one of the crazy mirrors in the Funhouse at the Fair.

It was just a child's notion, and by the summer that Harry came to be with us I wasn't a child any more and not a man either. If I remembered that idea at all it was something to laugh at. Still, like all the other cockeyed, cross-eyed visions from the knee-high world of children, it had some truth in its distortion.

Not a child any more and not yet a man. In the fall I would be sent back, according to the family custom still followed by those who could afford it, to military school. In that curious cold greenhouse the flowering from boy to man was supposed to be accomplished. I wasn't happy about it. I had been there. Suffered and survived. Conformed and thus gained some freedom. At least that was one lesson from the

35

world of men, though you either learned it by accident, tripped over the truth as you might bump into and fall over a piece of furniture in a dark, but known room, or you were hurt and broken. What happened was that you stifled your impulse to rebel and followed an urge to conform. Very slowly it dawned on you that you were now anonymous. Nobody knew who you really were. You were just another pale-faced, gray-uniformed body passing up and down the cold stone halls of the barracks named for an Episcopal bishop, standing in ranks, marching on the parade ground, or sitting in a classroom with your compass and sharp pencil trying to prove that Euclid was right. Meanwhile you, the real you, were far away and somewhere else. You pushed the flesh and bones that bore your name through a thousand motions and activities every day. In a while these became routine and habit, and you could prod yourself along, all the separate and integral parts, careless and thoughtless as a shepherd with a flock of calm sheep grazing. You were free as a bird or a beast. The rebels charged windmills, battered at closed doors and high walls with their bare heads and were always bloodied and always finally bowed. You never had to bow. Of course your body did obeisance to custom and ceremony. But while your flesh knelt before some honored institution your spirit was dancing jigs and horn-pipes and thumbing its nose at everything under the sun.

There was another lesson to be learned, not yet but soon after, as inevitable and abstract as those theorems and corollaries of Euclid: that the other survivors were doing exactly the same thing. That would be a chilly realization when you knew that all the others, like yourself, were ghosts in the flesh, countries and counties and continents populated by gray ghosts while, invisible, the world of spirits was a tumultuous chaos. Then you'd have to learn to live with that too.

36

But none of these things was much on my mind when Harry came to stay with us. I just thought that it would be good to have him around and show him things. I envied and admired him by that time. He had grown tall and slender and handsome. Everyone said he looked Spanish (the last of the Spanish blood in the family) and all agreed he was the best looking one in the whole family. He had his own car he had put together out of old parts from a junk yard, and he drove it down. (I still had a bike.) He brought guns and all kinds of fishing tackle with him. Up in his part of the state there was still lots of wild, wide, open country, and he had spent most of his spare time in the woods. When he arrived I helped him unload the car and carry all the stuff in the house and up to his room on the second floor. My father greeted him on the front porch and saw the rifles and the shotgun, and he didn't say anything but welcome.

When we got everything up to his room, Harry piled it all in a corner and flopped down on the big double bed and smoked. (I wasn't allowed to smoke yet.)

"Daddy must like you a lot," I said.

"How come? Why do you say that?"

"He doesn't allow any guns in the house. But he didn't say a word when he saw yours."

Harry laughed. "He doesn't care. He just feels *superior* and doesn't care."

"Oh, I don't think that's it."

"Or," Harry went on, ignoring my idea, "maybe he just feels sorry for me. That makes me sick. It's exactly the same thing as feeling superior."

"I just think he wants you to feel at home."

"Well, it's a damn good thing," Harry said. "If he said anything about my guns I would've turned right around and hopped in the car and left."

"Where would you go to?"

Everything I said seemed to tickle Harry. He laughed at that too.

"Somewhere. Oh, I'd go somewhere," he said. He bounced up and down on the bed and then turned over on his stomach. "You know? I think I'm going to like it here. This has got my room at home beat a mile."

We were off for a summer of it, it seemed. Harry had lots of tales and plots and plans and ideas. Harry was bored and restless, fidgety and as calm as a stone in the sun at the same time. Harry had caught tarpon all by himself off the east coast, and he had killed more than one buck in the woods. He was a strange and wonderful kind of blood kin to have. He could make you want to show him everything you cared about in the whole country, and as you were showing it to him you knew all the time he'd be scornful and either by laughter or silence make you ashamed of every bit of it and yourself. Beautiful things could turn shoddy and cheap from one of his skeptical glances. He could laugh about anything. He even got the giggles when we went to St. Luke's Cathedral for Holy Communion. He held it all back while we were still kneeling at the altar, but when we went out the side door to go back to our pew, he ducked in the dark little room where they keep the vestments for the acolytes and started to laugh.

"What's the matter?"

"I can't help it," he said. "I got to thinking that's probably the only way I'll get a drink the whole time I'm here."

"That's sacrilegious."

"So what?"

"Don't you care?"

"Listen," he said. "If God was to walk in this room right now, I'd thumb my nose at Him."

Harry was brave, there was no doubt about that. He would take any kind of a dare my friends and I could come up with.

He dived off the top of a high light-pole at Rock Springs and he didn't break his neck. He drove his car wide open up and down the main drag through all the red lights and the cops couldn't catch him. (Not *then*, anyway. They knew whose car it was all right.) He did whatever he felt like whenever he felt like it.

He used to talk a lot about wanting to be in the Army. (The real Army. He scorned military school.)

"I'll be glad when I can get in," he said. "I know everything there is about guns and I can really shoot a rifle."

The proof of that was that whenever he felt cranky and like being alone, he'd go down to the lake at the end of the street and shoot at snapping turtles. When they poked their little black heads above the surface he'd fire one shot and hit one most every time.

I thought it was fun to have him around.

That same summer Joe Childs came back from reform school. He was a lot older than we were, but he had been in the same grade with me all through the public schools until I went away to military school and he got sent off to the reform school at Raiford for trying to set fire to somebody's house. He was one of the barefooted, shambling, overage, shaggy-haired, snaggle-toothed, dull-eyed cracker boys, who always came to school in overalls and never took a bath. They brought their lunch in paper bags and ate outside under the trees by themselves instead of in the lunchroom where everybody else ate. Cornbread usually. They bullied everybody else, carried knives, were cruel to Negroes, cripples, stray dogs, and old maids. They smoked in the latrines. When they got caught at it the Principal beat them on the bare skin with a piece of rubber hose. But they were famous for never hollering or breaking into tears.

"*Him?* I don't pay him no never mind. *My* old man draws blood when *he* swings a strap."

39

Joe Childs was big and ugly and slow-witted. He had a lazy yellow smile all the time, but he could be cruel. When we were still in grammar school and his age and size made a lot more difference, he used to make some of us bring him a meat sandwich every day. If we didn't he beat us up. I used to beg my mother and Edna, the cook, for a meat sandwich. If they wouldn't make one for me I'd either have to play hookey that day or take a beating. I'd go dragging to school with my heart in my throat like a wad of sour grease and my feet like two heavy lead weights. It was hard to go ahead and go when you knew you were bound to take a beating.

Finally, after a long time of it, I broke down and told them why I had to have a meat sandwich every day.

My mother was really angry and all for telling the Principal, but the funny thing was that my father didn't get mad at all.

"That poor boy hasn't got anybody looking after him," he said. "Tell Edna to fix a meat sandwich every morning."

I'll never know, I guess, whether that was the right thing or not, or whether that was just feeling superior and sorry at the same time the way Harry said. At the time, anyway, it was a great relief. My father carefully explained to me that Joe Childs' father was a veteran of the First World War. He had been gassed and he couldn't do much work any more. His wife had run away and disappeared when Joe was still a baby. He drank a lot.

When Joe Childs got back from reform school, or anyway the first we knew about it was the day when some of us were out at the Old Fairgrounds playing ball. (Harry didn't come with us. He couldn't see any point in games.) Joe Childs came running up out of a pit they had dug there years before, before the Depression, to put in a big municipal swimming pool. All they did was dig a hole in the ground. There were two other guys running along with Joe Childs.

There were five of us, and I was standing with my back to the bushes around the pit knocking flies out to the others. I heard somebody or something thrashing in the bushes behind me and I twisted around to see what it was. And there stood Joe Childs, smiling that lazy yellow smile, and there were the two others, strangers to the town, on either side of him.

"Chunk me the ball." That was the first thing he said.

I threw it to him and he bounced it in his palm a few times and then put it in his pocket.

"All right," he said. "I'll take the bat too."

I wasn't going to give him the bat even if it meant a fight. He was big, but we had them five to three, and the other guys had run in from field and gathered around me.

"Don't you hear me, boy?"

I put the bat in my hands like a club.

"You'll have to take it if you want it."

All three of them reached in their pockets at one time and came up with big, long-bladed jackknives. I had had knives pulled on me before, and I was scared as soon as the sunlight hit the open blades and glanced off them brightly. All of them grinned at our surprise.

"Go on and give him the bat."

I handed it to him and he pushed me down.

"We don't want no kids from town coming out here and playing ball," he said. "You come out here again and we'll cut you wide open. Get!"

We turned around and started to walk across the field to where our bikes were parked, downcast and mad.

"Run, God damn you! Run!"

And we ran all the way to our bikes, hopped on, and pedaled away for all we were worth until we were out of sight.

I told Harry all about it that evening.

"You just let them walk over you like that?"

"What else could we do?"

"I'll tell you what you can do," he said. "You get another bat and a ball from somewhere and go back out there tomorrow afternoon."

"We couldn't do that."

"Don't worry," Harry said, laughing. "I'll come along too. Let's see if they'll try and pull a knife on *me*."

The next afternoon we piled into Harry's car and drove out to the lonely Old Fairgrounds. We started to play ball in the same spot. We played a little while, so tense and waiting for what we knew was going to happen we could hardly catch or hit the ball. Pretty soon, sure enough, the three of them came running out of the pit, blundering through the bushes like runaway animals. This time they had their knives out already.

"I thought I done told you all," Joe Childs said. He was red in the face he was so mad.

Harry came walking straight toward the three of them.

"What's the matter with you, waterhead?"

That made Joe Childs even madder. He *did* have a big head. He started for Harry, but before he could even move a couple of steps Harry calmly reached in his pocket and took out a little pistol. I didn't even know he had it with him. No wonder he was so sure of himself! He didn't wait or just wave it around either. When he pulled it out he shot— WHAM! (Every one of us jumped.)—about an inch or so in front of Joe Childs' bare foot. The three of them stopped like somebody had jerked them backwards on a leash. Joe Childs turned as pale as the belly of a catfish. One of his buddies broke out in a sweat all over and the other one wet his pants.

"Throw down them knives."

They dropped them in the grass.

"Okay," Harry said. "Let's all go down in the pit."

We picked up the knives and followed behind him. He marched them down in the pit and made them line up in a row with their hands up in the air. Just like the movies. We saw that they had built themselves a lean-to shack down there, and there were cans and bottles all around. They must have been living there.

"You know what you are?" Harry said.

They didn't say anything. The one who had wet his pants shook his head, but none of them said a thing.

"You're trash, white trash," he said. "I'd just as soon shoot you as not. Understand that?"

They all nodded.

"Now," he said. "All together: *We're trash! We're trash! We're trash!*"

They stood in front of him with their hands in the air and shouted over and over again that they were trash until Harry got tired of laughing and listening to them. He grabbed hold of my arm and pushed me right in front of Joe Childs.

"All right," he said. "Hit him."

I had been raised never to hit anyone first and especially somebody who couldn't hit you back. I couldn't do it. But Harry kept yelling in my ear until I finally hit him in the face.

"*Hit* him! I didn't say *tap* him. Hit him!"

I hit him a little harder. Joe Childs shook his head and had to spit on the ground. Harry kept on nagging at me until I hit the other two. The last I really teed-off on and he sat down. One by one we had to hit them, and after the first go-around we began to get in the mood for it. We were possessed by it. Round and around we went, hitting them until their faces were all cut and bruised and bloody, and they were begging us to quit. When they wouldn't get up off the ground to be hit again we kicked them until they would. We hit them until our hands hurt. When their faces got too bad we hit them in the stomach and the ribs. They got sick all over the ground and cried like babies.

In the end, once we had really got going, Harry had a hard time stopping us. They just lay on the ground and moaned. The strange thing was that all of us, who hadn't even dreamed of doing anything like that before, felt wild and exhilarated and good about it.

Harry kicked the lean-to over and we jumped up and down on it and smashed it to pieces. Then we piled everything they had on top of it and stuffed magazines and paper in wads underneath.

"You," Harry said to Joe Childs, prodding him with the point of his shoe. "Get up."

He struggled to his feet and moaned. He staggered and looked like a bear or a dog trying to walk on its hind legs, and we laughed at him.

"You're the one that plays with fire, ain't you?"

He kept both hands over his face and mumbled something.

Harry gave him a pack of matches and told him to start a fire. He knelt with trembling fingers and touched a match to the wadded paper. It caught and the dry wood caught too, and then there was a good crackling fire. After everything was burning good he made them empty their pockets and throw everything on the fire. Then we took them out of the pit and made them run, across the fairgrounds and away from town. They were weak, running and falling down. We yelled and hooted after them, and Harry shot at them a couple of times, over their heads. They picked up a great burst of speed when he did that, and we got to laughing so hard we fell on the ground and rolled over and over.

Then we climbed in Harry's car and drove it as fast as it would go, wildly, out in the country and all over the county. We laughed and sang and joked. It was just like being drunk.

44

It was only late that night when I was alone in my room trying to get to sleep that I started to feel real bad about it. I got up and went down the hall to Harry's room and woke him up to talk about it. He sat right up when I touched him, switched on the bedside light and smoked and listened to me. He laughed at my doubts and shame.

"They asked for it, didn't they, pulling knives like that?"

"Sure," I said. "It isn't that simple, though. It isn't that I feel sorry for them or anything. They probably would do the same to us if they could. It's just I didn't know I had it in me to act like that. We all went kind of crazy. I didn't know I could do like that. I didn't know I could enjoy it."

The answer he gave me has stuck, because, in a curious way, in the next years the whole world seemed to be asking itself the same question and getting the same answer. And once tasted, that doubt and shame is with you, on your tongue always. Harry puffed on his cigarette and looked at me. For once he wasn't smiling.

"Now you know," he said.

That ought to be the end of it, but it isn't. I don't know how I would have ended up feeling about Harry and myself if he had stayed on for the rest of the summer. I never found out. A few days later he got a telegram that his father was in a bad way, and he had to go to Baltimore. My father bought him a ticket on the plane and he left. And I didn't see him again. His father lived on through the summer and didn't die until I was already back at military school and couldn't come back for the funeral. I wrote him that I was sorry to hear about that, but I didn't get any answer.

Of course I thought about him and that one terrible thing we had done a lot. Since he wasn't there any more except as I chose to remember him, I usually made him the villain of the story, the one who had put us up to it, rather than simply the one who had made me see the potential of evil and

45

violence in myself. For which, I guess, I should have been grateful.

Then along towards Christmas, not too long before vacation, I got a letter from home which said that Harry had accidently killed himself on a hunting trip. That seemed strange because he knew so much about guns and how to take care of himself. And I knew that the truth must be that he had killed himself, though I couldn't have said why. Except that maybe he knew too much about himself and other people too early.

But the strangest thing of all was how I felt when I surmised this. At first I was just plain numb, the way you always are about confronting a brute and sudden fact. But then one night after taps and after the midnight bed check when the beam of a flashlight crisscrossed our tranquil faces, I sat up in the cold dark and cried silently. It was a great deep loss to me all of a sudden. As much as I hated the memory of what had happened in the summer and still burned with shame at the injustice of his scorn and laughter, I felt that something had been taken away, stolen from me, that in some wordless way he had cheated me. I wept like a woman deceived and forsaken by a lover.

Then I felt better and turned over and went to sleep.

46

the victim

At first there was an odor in the dry and dusty woods. Their nostrils caught it and quivered. Then it was in the leaves, a flicker of something unexpected like a sourceless shaft of light or the swift passage of a bird nearby, unseen. By the time they heard it unmistakably, the sparkling rush and white roar of water on rocks, they were already running. They blundered among the trees, tripped over roots and stones and fallen branches, thrashed like swimmers as they ran, and plunged headlong down a sudden steep slope, falling, rolling, bruised and bleeding from the rocks and the gnash of underbrush, but always rising and running on until they came to the edge of the mountain stream, fell on their bellies, pushed head and shoulders into its thrilling current,

47

and gulped at it. The cold water was as cruel as fire to their parched tongues, cracked lips, their dusty throats.

They had been without water all day long.

Side by side they lay in the coarse sand and gravel, heads and shoulders thrust into the stream, the young man in khaki and the fat man, middle-aged, wearing the gray work uniform of the State Prison Farm. Almost at the same instant, like puppets, they raised their dripping heads and looked at each other and started to laugh. The cold water ran down them as, half-raised, they looked deeply into each other's eyes, staring with the intensity of lovers. The young man cupped a handful of water and splashed the other. The fat man, using his hands like little paddles, splashed back, and in a moment they were lost in a bright storm of splashing, wordless and wild.

They might almost have embraced then, they were so close, but the rifle lay between them like a sword.

Spent, they rolled over on their backs and looked into the bowl of the sky, blue as the heart of a flame with, here and there, the immaculate sculptured clouds of midsummer. A way off, behind them, back where they had come from, a buzzard circled in a slow lazy arc, then vanished behind the trees.

"I'm going to take off my shoes," the fat man said. "The hell with it. I'm going to pleasure myself."

He sat up, bending over the sag and bulk of his belly and, groaning a little, began to unlace his high-top work shoes. The young man grunted and looked at him, and it was then that the blued glint of the rifle barrel caught his eye. Very slowly while the fat man struggled with the laces of his shoes, the young man's hand, poised high on its fingertips like a large, lazy spider, moved toward the rifle. When the fat man seized a shoe with both hands to tug it off, the young man snatched at the rifle, rolled away, cocked it in the blurred

48

moment that he was rolling, sat up, and snapped the safety off. The little click that the safety made might as well have been thunder. The fat man froze with one limp shoe dangling like a small dead animal in his hand, still not looking at the young man, but knowing what had happened. His whole body seemed to turn to wax at once. Face and muscle began to melt, and he let the shoe slip from his fingers. Only his head turned, sad-eyed and hurt, the lips trembling like elastic stretched too taut, the rolls of fat below his face, where the tanned neck joined the fish-belly whiteness of his body in a ragged little horizon, shook. The young man saw sweat pop out all over his face at once and shine like a thick coat of grease.

The young man felt his own lips form a slight smile.

"I'll take the knife too," he said.

The fat man began to cry at this, his opulent flesh from head to toe shuddering and tears running down his cheeks.

"You got the gun," he said. "I mean you got everything now. Why take the knife too? If you have the gun, what harm is there in a little jackknife?"

"Give it to me," the young man said. "And give it to me right. I want it."

The fat man mumbled to himself and dug in his pockets. His hand came up with the jackknife in it, and he edged his hand forward, palm up, fingers slack and useless, the knife resting lightly in his palm.

"Just drop it in the sand. *That's* right."

The knife fell and the fat man wiped his face with his sleeve. He had stopped crying now. He rubbed his sleeve across his face, and gradually his face seemed to take a shape and color again. Even his eyes brightened.

"I should have known," he said. "I just got so thirsty I couldn't even think. I guess I got careless."

"Oh, you've been careless," the young man said. "Last

49

night, the night before, you dozed off and I could've taken the gun then. I could have jumped you anytime in the woods."

"Don't forget I had the knife too. Don't forget that."

"You're a damn fool," he said. "I could've wrung your neck like an old stewing hen anytime I wanted to. And it wouldn't even be a crime. Just good riddance."

The fat man swallowed hard and quick lines of puzzlement troubled his forehead.

"If that's the truth, why didn't you? If you could, why didn't you? That's what I'd like to know."

"I don't really know," the young man said. "I just must have wanted to wait you out."

"Hah!"

"No, I'm serious. I knew if I waited long enough you'd forget yourself. You'd start to want something so bad you'd forget all about everything, what we were doing, where we were going, the whole works. People are like that. As soon as they start to want something they got one-track minds."

"You don't care much for other people. You got a fine contempt for them."

"Don't feel bad about it," the young man said. "I waited so long, I got so thirsty, I pretty near forgot myself. Now just don't you move."

He stood up and felt for the knife one-handed, the other hand holding the rifle, his index finger hooked over the trigger, the rifle hip-high, pointed straight at the body of the fat man, his eyes never leaving the other's. When his hand found the knife, he eased it into his pocket, then he moved back and away up the slope, crabwise, until he came to a tree he could lean against.

"That was all right," he said. "Now go ahead. Go ahead and soak your feet if you want to."

He leaned against the rough bark of the pine tree, wriggling his shoulders to scratch his back, smelling the piney green sweetness, cradling the cool rifle in his arms; and the other turned his back to him and sat on a flat rock, dangling his bare feet in the water. The fat man wiggled his toes in the water like a child.

"You're a pleasure-loving old bastard," the young man said. "How did you ever stand it in jail?"

The fat man didn't answer. He turned his head and grinned briefly. He finished washing his feet and letting them dry in the sun and air. He put on his socks carefully, smoothing the wrinkles out, and he squatted on his bulging haunches and laced up his shoes, tied them in a neat firm knot. Then he stood up.

"All right," he said. "What now?"

"I dropped my pack up on the hill when we started running. I don't know just where, but it can't be far," the young man said. "Let's us stroll up there and pick up my pack and my canteen. Then we'll come back here and fix us something to eat. Unless maybe you aren't hungry?"

"I'm hungry all right."

"Lead off, fat man. I'm right behind you."

In a while they had a twig and brush fire going down by the stream. The fat man crouched beside it, stirring the twigs, blowing on the flames. The young man sat back against the tree and watched. They had two cans of beans, a little can of potted meat, some bacon, and a few pieces of bread. The fat man strung the bacon on a forked green stick and held it over the flame. Grease spat into the fire and the flame danced. There was a good crackling sound and the good smell of bacon cooking.

"If you hadn't of been in such a big hurry," the young man said, "we'd be all right. We could've brought along my pup tent and the rest of my stuff."

"We never would've made it this far with all that," the fat

man said. "We come a pretty good ways. I expect we're in Tennessee already."

"No we're not. We're still in North Carolina. Tennessee is a ways yet."

"I haven't heard the dogs all day. I haven't heard a single sound of dogs."

"I expect you will before long."

The fat man took the bacon off the forked stick and folded half the strips into a piece of bread. He came toward the young man, bent over, deferential, cautious, and handed him the sandwich. Then he backed down the slope again to the fire and fixed his own. He held it tight in his hands so that the grease could soak evenly into his piece of bread. Then he began to nibble at it in quick little bites like a squirrel with a nut.

"Stick the beans in the fire."

"How we going to get the cans open?"

"I'll let you use the knife."

"Both cans? Don't you think we better save one?"

"What for? Like you said we're almost to Tennessee." The young man grinned and tossed the knife to him.

When the beans were warm, they ate them with their fingers, licking the sweet brown sauce so as not to lose a drop. They split the other piece of bread to wipe the cans clean. The can of potted meat remained unopened.

"Go ahead and have it," the young man said. "You're a big man. You need it worse than I do."

The fat man opened the can. Looking up, he saw the young man was busy mopping his can of beans with the piece of bread. He kept his eyes on the young man and very slowly slipped the knife back into his pocket. The young man made no movement.

"Look in my pack," he said. "There's a pack of cigarettes and some matches. Help yourself and throw it to me."

52

They sat where they were, facing each other, contented and refreshed, and they smoked.

A few days before, the young man had seen the fat man for the first time. The young man came down a road in the mountains with his pack and roll on his back and his rifle slung over his shoulder. It was towards evening and he came on a gang of prisoners working on the road. First he saw the guard with a shotgun, sitting on a canvas camp stool under a khaki umbrella, his pith helmet propped back on his head, his shirt open all the way down the front. Then he saw the prisoners nearby. In their gray uniforms, in the clouds of dust their picks and shovels stirred up, they themselves seemed to be composed entirely of dust, to be walking and working piles of animated dust. He had the feeling then that if either he or the guard—who nodded with just a slight tip of his head to salute their mutual freedom—that if either one of them took a deep breath and blew, the whole gang of prisoners would disappear into just nothing and nowhere like a dandelion or a thistleweed. The prisoners did not stop working as he passed between them—they were on both sides of the road—and no head raised, no eye, accusing or pitiful or serious, met his. He heard a kind of low moan or sigh which, as he listened, he took to be a song. But it was late in the day for singing.

He had nearly passed by them when he encountered the fat man. The fat man came out of the bushes onto the road, bearing a wooden water bucket, and his uniform was astonishingly clean. He set the bucket down and unfolded a large colored handkerchief on the road in front of the young man, without a word offering him for sale the things which the prisoners had made—rings made out of toothbrush handles, bracelets made of bent spoons, and even a drawing

53

or kind of painting on a piece of white cloth, made with ink and clay and some sort of coloring, maybe the juice of wild berries. It showed Calvary with Christ crucified between the two thieves, and, as the young man stooped to look at it more closely, he smiled to see that the artist had lavished most of his detail and color and attention on the thieves. They were naked and identical, crudely done, but clearly the same man, based on some real flesh and form. The Christ was eyeless and vague as a store-window mannequin. The young man almost decided to buy it, but when he rose to ask how much it was worth, he saw that the man's eyes were looking past him, fixed with a kind of obsessive glint on the high-powered rifle. He dropped the cloth from his hands and stepped past the fat man, touching him flank to flank for one instant, feeling the heat of his body, smelling his short, sour breath.

That night he slept in his bedroll, alone in the deep woods. Near dawn he woke from a bad dream, a dream of running from something, a dream where gates and doors refused to open and all roads were a treadmill in reverse, to see the fat man standing over him holding the rifle. In the faint first light that came through the gloom of trees he could see the fat man smiling. He rose, still half-asleep, and picked up his pack. The fat man motioned with the rifle, and he walked off into the woods with the fat man following close behind. Later in the gray deceptive light of dawn, a light like a splash of dirty water, they first heard the dogs.

Now the fat man was sitting by the ruins of the fire, the tin corpses of their meal. He was blowing smoke rings, large ones with little ones inside.

"I just thought of something," the young man said. "You could've killed me. You could've killed me right at first while I was still asleep."

"Sure, I *could*," the fat man said. "But what good would it do me?"

"Yeah, they hang you for murder."

"That's right, they surely do that," the fat man said, and he giggled.

"You could've sneaked away. I could have slept right on and just woke up without my rifle."

"Maybe. Maybe so."

The young man put his cigarette into the sand, buried it neatly. He was, even now, dirty, unshaven, hatless, tired, surprisingly neat for a man out of doors. He thought about it.

"You were just scared," he said finally. "You were too scared to run away alone."

"Maybe," the fat man said, equally thoughtful. "Maybe that's the case."

"You *would've* killed me, but you were scared. You *would've* left me alone, but you were scared."

"Maybe that's right."

"You know one thing I can't stand about people—or maybe I ought to say one of the *things* I can't stand—it's fear. People who get scared make me sick."

"You don't scare? You weren't scared when you woke up and saw me there?"

"No, I wasn't scared."

"You would've been wise to be a little bit scared. Somebody else might have killed you."

The young man shrugged. "Well, here I am. I got the rifle, and I'm not any worse off for a walk through the woods. What about you? You ought to be scared now."

"I'm scared."

"If they take you back, they're going to take the bullhide to you. They're going to lock you in a sweat box for a while, and when you come out—if you come out—you'll never be a trusty again. They'll have you swinging a pick, full time, in the hot sun."

"I can't help being fat."

"You make me sick to my stomach," the young man said. "Bury that stuff."

He pointed with the rifle barrel to the two cans, and the little can, so cleaned inside they shone, and to the ashes of the fire. The fat man kneeled and scooped a hole in the sand. He buried the cans and the ashes under a little mound.

"What did you ever *do* to end up in jail? What did you have guts enough to do?"

Still kneeling before him, the fat man laughed.

"I got involved in this rape case. I mean it wasn't exactly rape when it happened, but it was her word against mine."

"I might have known it would be something like that. What were you doing before you got into trouble?"

"You might say I was a kind of a travelling preacher. I had the power of healing, too, for a while. But the Lord took it back."

"A kind of a *hypocrite* would be a better word for it. Preach one thing and practice another. And then get caught in a rape." The young man laughed bitterly.

"You don't allow much for other folk's weakness."

"Why should I?"

"Listen, the Good Book says we supposed to love each other. Now, if you love somebody, you surely going to tolerate a little weakness."

"I'll give it right back to you," the young man said. "The Bible says love they neighbor as theyself, right?"

"That's right."

"Well, then, Mr. Convict Jailbird Fatman—"

"I got a name."

"Well, I don't want to hear it," the young man said. "Now, my point is this. If you *don't* love yourself, then what?"

56

"Oh, you *bound* to love yourself."

"Just suppose you don't. Just suppose for the sake of arguing you *hate* yourself."

"I don't follow you," the fat man said.

"If you hate yourself, you got the right to hate everybody else in the world."

"I just don't understand what you're talking about."

"The hell with it," the young man said. "Let it be."

Just then, far off, faint in the waning afternoon, they could hear the clear belling sounds of the dogs. The sounds were far behind them, but they could tell that the dogs were on the right trail. They stood up simultaneously and stared at each other, unsmiling.

"I guess you better get started," the young man said.

"You going to let me go? You going to let me be?"

"You better get going before I change my mind."

"Ain't you coming too?"

"For God's sake why?" the young man said. "I've gone along far enough with you."

The fat man stood, head down, shifting his weight from one leg to the other like a small boy. When he looked up again there was a shy womanly softness in his face. He fumbled in a pocket and pulled out the cloth he had offered for sale.

"You can have it," he said. "I did it by myself, color and all."

He spread the cloth on the sand, smoothed it, then he turned and began to wade across the stream.

"You better go with the water a ways," the young man said. "So they'll lose the scent."

The fat man nodded without looking back. He went downstream awkwardly, wading in the knee-deep water, picking his way among the rocks. Once he stumbled on a wet stone and fell, but he struggled up to his feet and kept going.

"You hypocrite bastard," the young man yelled after him. "You've still got the knife."

The fat man stopped. He still did not look back, but he nodded and reached in his pocket for the knife.

"You can have it back," he shouted back over the noise of the water. "I don't need it. I'll give it back."

"Keep it. Go on and keep it now."

Then the fat man started to run in the water. The young man stood up. He dug the butt of the rifle into the hollow of his shoulder, sighted down the barrel, and fixed the gray diminishing back of the fat man in the tense slim V of the front sight. He took a deep breath, let out a little, and then held the rest. The barrel was steady. Gently he took up the slack in the trigger and began a smooth squeeze. He saw the fat man twitch and tumble with a great white splash, and then he heard the sharp report of the rifle thunder in the ravine and echo, dying away, in the woods. He heard the little *chink* of the ejected shell as it bounced off the rock by his feet. He stooped and policed it up, buried it under the sand. He picked up the picture and folded it and put it in his shirt pocket. Then he walked back to the pine tree and sat down and closed his eyes, listening to the dogs as they came, waiting.

the confidence man

The motorcycle, flaring a roar of sound behind its improbable, tilting forward rush, was the first sign of the change. Through years the summer visitors to Gulfport had become accustomed to the spectacle of Miss Alma, prim on her bicycle, twisting in and out of the shiny herd of traffic on the main street, Palm Boulevard, and precariously descending the slight slope down to the wharf where the Fish Market used to be. There she'd dismount, carefully lock her bicycle, and be seen, a slight gray-haired woman in a high-collared cotton dress, moving among the tall tanned fishermen, boys with their eyes still squinted against the shifting winds and the shiny brass of the waves, awkward and heavy-footed as ducks on dry land. There amid the clatter of unloading, the sagging nets hoisting the squirm and silver of the catch from

59

the boats, the coarse laughter, the rich odor of the deep sea, she'd be like a thin ghost edging her way to examine, haggle, poke, and finally buy a single fish for dinner. She was the only person in the world still allowed to market right there where the boats came in instead of uptown at the new Fish Market. Nobody had the heart or the inclination to tell her that long ago all that had changed. Would it have made any difference if they *had* told her? Not a bit. She'd stiffen and go right on about her business. She'd buy a fish and one of the fishermen would produce a paper bag from somewhere and write the price, still the same price, on it with a black grease pencil. She'd open her formidable purse, rummage, count the money out. He'd pocket the coins and, more than likely, tip his hat.

"Thank you very much, Miss Alma," he'd say as if she had conferred a special favor on him by the purchase.

She'd mount her bicycle and pedal away. The summer visitors found it very amusing. It was almost absurd enough to make up for the fact that she was anything but helpless when it came to renting the summer cottages she owned along the beach. She made them pay for the privilege of renting a beach cottage in her town with a fine view of her ocean. When it came to real estate, not the least, most subtle variation in the national economic structure escaped her attention.

Miss Alma lived in a fine old Florida house, long, high-ceilinged, rambling, with only a bit of the roof visible above a green jungle of pines and palms and live oaks, ragged shrubs like wild beasts crouching on what had been a lawn. You passed the driveway with its peeling signboard, *Capt. T. R. Drinkwater, Esq.*, but you didn't go in. If you had business you conducted it in a paintless lean-to at the edge of the driveway that looked like a child's lemonade stand. Which in fact was what it was. When The Old Fraud died, Miss Alma made it her office.

60

"Didn't I build this myself?" she'd holler. "Shoo, children, shoo!"

Sure enough she had built it. She had sat there, longer than was respectable some said, selling lemonade to passersby, unsmiling, condescending, until her mother died and she was busy from then on leaping about the house like an acrobat to the raging commands of the Captain. That he was mad, that he had never been to sea as the captain of anything, tugboat or *Titanic*, did not lessen the authority of the myth he had found for himself, believed in with all his heart until, at last, even Gulfport accepted it without question. You could hear him and he *did* sound like a foghorn in foul weather. You might have seen him then on the sidewalk, leaning down as if he were bucking the breeze of a gale, rolling-gaited in the plenty of space that opened in front of him without a whisper or the raising of an eyebrow no matter how crowded the time or the day, talking to no one but himself. To be in the real-estate business! To be a seaman condemned to the parcelling out of little pieces of dry land to a flock of ridiculous spineless figures in piratical costumes who thought the Gulf of Mexico was something to look at, for children to splash brightly in, to cast a fishing line into or to sail on, safe and clumsy in their rented boats, rented from him, cramming the pure calm of the bay with the cursed diagonals of their sails! It's no wonder there was a strong odor of bourbon whiskey in his wake. No wonder the children followed behind, shrill and active like a flight of gulls. And naturally everybody said, "Poor Alma."

Yes, no one was ready for the motorcycle. That day the fishing boats churned into the little bay, the tourists assembled with cameras, and the gulls coaxed with bleak cries overhead. One or two heads might have turned casually to the

61

place where the road comes into view to see her strict, indignant pedalling. Then they heard the motorcycle. It careened into sight, skidding on the curve, a lank man in a straw hat holding the long-horned handle bars, and behind him, clinging to his waist, unabashed, Miss Alma, her skirt misbehaving in the wind and her laughter as naked and shrill as a young girl's. They were so still they might have been a photograph themselves, those tourists with cameras, when the motorcycle shot onto the dock, came to a screeching halt. The tall man rolled down his pants legs, took off the goggles he'd been wearing, cocked his straw hat at a wry angle, and, openly, for all the world to see, bought two nice bluefish while Miss Alma, breathless still from the wild ride, held his motorcycle for him. The fisherman even had *to make change* for him. When he walked back to her with the paper bag, the taps of his heels clicked arrogantly on the dock. He rolled up his pants legs again, revealing red silk socks and a wide garter. He put the goggles on, adjusted them, pulled his hat far down over his ears, and stamped down on the starter. And they were off in a coughing growl, propelled out of sight at unbelievable speed, never even slowing at the curve.

It was one of the fishermen who spoke first.

"He's from Georgia," he said. "I can always tell a Georgia accent."

"Pocket full of money. Did you see all those bills?"

"I didn't know Miss Alma had any family in Georgia."

"As far as I know, she don't," someone said. "Anyway, that fellow don't have the Drinkwater nose."

"Might be on the Cawley side."

"Doubt it."

It wasn't long before everybody was concerned about poor Miss Alma. It didn't take long to figure out what *he* was up to. What if he *did* have such fine manners, would move aside for a lady on the sidewalk with even the subtle indication of

62

an old-fashioned bow, tipping his straw hat high and wide.

What if he had an alligator wallet crisp with the money he was quick to spend everywhere, for flowers, for a bottle of wine, for a Brownie camera and several rolls of film, for a box of fine linen handkerchiefs, initialed? If his summer suits were neat and clean, creased to perfection, if his pointed tapping two-toned shoes gleamed with white and brown where they ought to, there was nevertheless no doubt that he was an Opportunist.

Larry Thompson, the plain-clothes policeman, patted his stomach and noted that this Mr. Hunter from Atlanta, Georgia, was a type well known to him.

"You can see him by the battalion at most any race track," he said. "I expect if you was to turn him upside down and give him a fair shake there'd be a regular shower of ticket stubs."

"It's a shame," everybody was saying, "to see a sweet, lonely, eccentric woman like Miss Alma taken advantage of."

At any rate, whatever was being said, there he was all smiles, bug-eyed in goggles, Miss Alma likewise smiling, zooming around the countryside on the devilish machine. They were seen everywhere together. They appeared together one fine day on the beach. Who can honestly remember seeing Miss Alma on the beach? But there they were with a bright umbrella and a striped beach ball that bounced like a joyful planet above the clear bells of her laughter. Oh yes, and she had been heard whistling, both of them whistling what might have been almost any tune as they lunged past baffled spectators in lean profile on the motorcycle.

"I'll keep my eye on that fellow," promised Everett Fairweather, the lawyer. If something, something that we all expected, happened, he'd know first.

He would have had a hard time if he meant this literally. They were all over the county. They were seen bidding at

63

an auction, right in the midst of the tourists. Someone with a pair of binoculars and the time to use them swore he saw the two of them heeling along in a swift white tack in a cat-boat on the bay.

"It's dangerous for a woman of middle age to carry on that way," began to be the sentiment among the women.

This seemed to be confirmed by what happened at the El Tropitan Nightclub. They were there too, all right, the report was, starting the evening with cocktails and a rock lobster dinner, oblivious of any eyebrows. They stayed on for an evening of it, and he became expansive, hiring the orchestra to play a medley of waltzes for her, having their picture taken a half-dozen times, ordering the tall, ice-packed, colored drinks that put the bartender into a sweaty frenzy. They laughed and he waved his hands grandiloquently, his diamond ring flashing in the light, as he told her stories. He tried on her glasses, made faces for her, and they sang loudly and off key without much provocation. It might, folks said, have gone on marvelously forever if she hadn't slipped and, head over heels no less, fallen with a memorable clatter in the midst of the dance floor while he was teaching her the mambo.

It was at this point that Lawyer Fairweather decided to step boldly forward. He arranged for a little talk with Mr. Hunter. And so, they say, the two of them sat in Fair-weather's office above the bank, the lawyer peering behind thick lenses at his prey, trying, in all fairness, to conceal his stern distaste. They talked for a while of this and that, feeling their way like crabs in a wavering submarine light. This gentleman from Georgia spun his fine straw hat like a gypsy's tambourine on his index finger while he spoke a little and listened more.

"About Miss Alma—" Fairweather finally began.

"The flower of the state of Florida," Hunter interrupted.

"That may be. There may be truth in that," the lawyer said. "She is my client, however, and I have the duty and pleasure of protecting her interests."

"I should say so," Hunter said.

"Now, Mr. Hunter, you've been most kind to the lady during this summer season—"

"I've done nothing at all."

"On the contrary. You've squired her around. You've offered her a kind of joy and pleasure she's usually been deprived of by virtue of her position in this town."

"Really, I have done nothing at all," Hunter said, modestly enough, staring at the sharp points of his shoes.

"It isn't often that a woman of middle age has the good fortune of an admirer years younger than herself."

"What are years, after all?" Hunter said in a whisper. "Alma has the spirit of a thoroughbred."

Fairweather winced at the allusion to the race track and bore down.

"And where will it all be at the end of the summer season?"

Hunter smiled broadly, triumphantly, spun the hat like a potter's wheel on his finger.

"Who knows?" he said. "Who can tell?"

"I'll be frank with you," the lawyer said. "I don't know for sure what you're up to, but I know you're up to something and I mean to tell you that I intend to protect my client."

"Indeed!" Hunter said, rising, nodding a parody of his sidewalk bow. "I can't say I thank you for your concern, though I thank you enough for being honest with me. Honesty is not to be despised, never, not even when its advocate is no gentleman."

So in a crisp huff he was gone and Fairweather was left to consider, puzzled, the neat rhythm of the tapped heels as they clicked down the hall. He spun his swivel chair around and looked through the window as Hunter, stiff-backed as a cadet, bowed his bow for the ladies, smiled his smile, and mounted the waiting motorcycle, so indignant, it seemed, at the suggestion that his motives were not wholly honorable that he forgot to roll up his trousers or put on his goggles.

Fairweather decided to give him a week before he approached Miss Alma on the delicate subject. A week was too long. By the time he'd dressed in a dark suit and slicked down his hair and was walking up the quiet dust of the driveway to call on the lady, the other one, irresponsible, yet shrewd as a cat, had vanished into thin air. The lawyer arrived at least in time to console. He sat stiffly in the living room, vaguely afraid of the close fragility of old things around him, and listened to the sad, inevitable tale of how the confidence man had roared away on his motorcycle, his alligator wallet bulging with new money—not *all* of it, of course, but all that had been hidden even from the lawyer's knowledge in a copper pitcher for years and years, back to the days of the lemonade stand.

"It was money that I had secreted from Father and from you as well," she said simply.

He decided he would have felt better, more at ease, if she hadn't been so tearless, rational, unperturbed (the women would say, and do, *unrepentant*). She asked him not for pity, even advice. She was just telling him what had happened.

"I'm sorry, Miss Alma, very sorry."

"Sorry? Why, Everett, what is there to be sorry about? I was duped out of my money by a clever and charming man. Oh he certainly was *that*—not clever I mean, not terribly clever—but charming, oh yes in his own way, quite a charming man."

"Well, we'll certainly catch up with him sooner or later."

"I think not," she said, standing up. "I rather hope not. That makes me feel a little sad. What would a man like Mr. Rodney Hunter, if that *is* his name, do in jail?"

At the door she gave him her hand and smiled.

"Do you know," she said, "it's going to be a little difficult to go back to my bicycle again. There was such a breeze and such a sound. There was so much speed on the motorcycle."

"The bike's a lot safer," he said. "You're more likely to get where you're going even if it takes a little longer."

"Oh yes," she said. "But not nearly as much fun. I may even buy myself a motorcycle. Do you know how to drive one, Everett? Could you teach me? Have you ever been on one?"

"No ma'am," he said quickly, and he hurried away down the still drive.

tIme of BItteR chIlòRen

The truck slowed to a hissing stop on the shoulder of the highway. The driver left the engine running. He pushed back away from the wheel, yawned and stretched, and, seeing that the man next to him in the cab was still sound asleep, hunched up in a small round ball of himself like a sleeping animal, he reached across and touched him lightly on the shoulder to wake him. At the touch the man uncoiled and sat up straight—alert, tense, red-eyed, and suspicious.

"This is far as I go," the driver said. "I'm turning north."

"You just going to dump me out here right in the middle of nowhere?"

"You suit yourself," the driver said. "Stay with me if you want to end up in Knoxville."

"I ain't *bound* for Knoxville. I'm headed south."

"That's what I thought you said," the driver said, grinning, easy. He was a big man, gentle in the knowledge of his own strength and power. "You already told me you was going south."

The small man squinted at him, and his sharp rodent's face worked itself into a mask of fine wrinkles, sly and dangerous.

"Why do I have to get out then? It's cold and lonesome up here in the mountains. Ain't nobody else on the road. What are you trying to *do* to me?"

The very idea made the driver laugh.

"Like I say, you can ride all the way to Knoxville if you want to. Suit yourself."

"You'll be going the wrong direction."

"From here on I will."

"Godamnit!" the little man said. "Don't that beat all?"

The driver was still more tickled than anything else, but he looked at his watch to see how much time he was wasting. It was past midnight already. He was going to have to put down a heavy foot on the gas as it was.

"Would you just turn a man loose in open country? There's probably wild animals and Lord knows what else up here. You'd just stop your truck and make a fellow get out and shiver in the cold?"

"I didn't tell you to get out yet, but I'm just fixing to."

"See there? See what I'm talking about? You don't give a hoot. What happened to all the charity in the world?"

"My charity, such as it is, goes as far as this turn off. I guess I'm through talking. Time to get off."

The driver shoved a long arm around behind the little man who had backed himself up against the cab door like a cornered animal. The man twitched and winced away from the arm as if he were dodging a blow, but the driver merely flicked the door handle and pushed it open. Then he had to be quick. The little man with all his weight against the door would have pitched out of the high cab if the driver hadn't seized him in a tight grip. For an instant they were locked there in a reluctant embrace.

"I guess somebody will be coming along pretty soon," the driver said.

"Who would stop and give *me* a ride?"

"What are you complaining about? *I* give you a ride, didn't I? You're just as bad as an old woman."

The driver shook his head, dismay now added to his natural curiosity. He refused to let himself be moved or troubled by the tears that began to roll down the little man's cheeks, large tears silently falling from the red-rimmed, blood-shot, phlegm-colored eyes, making jagged streaks along his dusty face.

"I see you've made up your mind," he said to the driver at last. "Invincible ignorance, I call it. Well, could you do me one thing?"

"What's that?"

"Lemme have a couple of cigarettes and a pack of matches."

The driver sighed with relief. He hadn't been able to guess what was coming next, and anyway this was going to make it simple and final. He took the half-empty pack from his pocket and fumbled for matches.

"Here," he said. "Keep the pack. I got another one."

The little man took them with his left hand, still keeping the other one out of sight as he had all along, jammed in his pants pocket. No "thank you," nothing. Just took the pack of cigarettes and the matches in his free left hand, slipped side-wise off the seat and dropped down to the ground. The driver had to reach all the way across and pull the door to. He shifted into low and pulled the big truck off the shoulder and back onto the road, made his turn and drove north.

70

For a moment he thought about it. Then he laughed out loud to himself.

"It does beat all," he said, "the way some people you run into these days act."

Then, with all that over and done with, he started thinking about the diner up the road, up near Knoxville where he would treat himself to a great big breakfast. There were a couple of cute little waitresses who worked there, and you could joke around with them if you felt like it. Driving a truck on long hauls wasn't such a lonesome job as a man might think.

The small man left behind stood in the middle of the road, stamping his feet in a fierce little dance, partly against the sudden chill of the night after the close warmth of the cab, partly out of an excess of puzzled frustration. He watched the red taillights of the truck and trailer vanish into the dark, swallowed whole. He spat on the road and cursed the driver and the truck and all Creation. Clenching his fist he felt the crackle of the cellophane on the half-empty pack of cigarettes and relaxed, feeling in the privacy of the dark a slow, sly grin forming itself on his lips.

He moved off the road, hopped lightly over a yawning ditch, sat down on the other side and dangled his legs. Expertly with his left hand he opened the pack of paper matches, folded one match back, struck it and lit a cigarette, staring into the blue heart of the little flame, letting his cupped palm feel the warmth of it until the match was burned almost down to the end. He puffed and blinked and let his eyes become accustomed to the dark again. Gradually the stars grew bright and the bulked shapes of the mountains loomed like huge, crouching beasts around him. He hunched

down as small as he could, as if to draw in against the dark
and the cold, as if somehow to conserve and protect, like the
cupped match flame he had stared at, the invisible heat of
his body and soul. He was like a drab little sparrow there. He
smoked and chuckled to himself.

"Well," he said, "if worse comes to worse, you could always get yourself a job as a scarecrow."

The picture of himself in a lonely field, arms outstretched,
scaring the crows away, tickled him no end.

Then, more sober, shouting into the dark: "You foxed him!
You foxed the fool out of half a pack of ready-made cigarettes!"

Lee Southgate was already on the road at that time. He was
driving fast because he had some business in eastern Tennessee in the morning, and he wasn't sleeping well in hotels and
motels anyway. He had stopped once, well east of Ashville,
and had an order of bacon and eggs and toast and coffee,
even though he hadn't been the least bit hungry. A travelling
man just had to stop every so often to get the feel of solid
ground under his feet again, the earth he spent so much of
his waking time and energy lightly skimming and scorning.
Like a dainty-legged waterbug swift across the surface of a
pond, he thought. Sometimes, for no special need or reason,
you had to light somewhere and take a look around.

So he stopped at the roadside diner, knowing the long,
winding, lonely drive through the mountains lay in dark
ambush ahead of him. He had eaten, played the juke box,
talked a while with the waitress and shown her the snapshots
in his wallet, pictures of his wife, his two young children, his
dog, and his new ranch-style house in the Whispering Pines
subdivision. It had been a nice time. The waitress was big,

72

plain, and sympathetic, motherly. He always got along easy with big, plain women.

Lee Southgate was a salesman for a sporting goods firm. He made a good living at it, but his territory in this part of the country had to be large. He was on the road a lot of the time and it was hard on him, wore him down. He was a natural salesman, much the same as some are natural actors; selling came easy to him; but the trips alone, the vague gaps of time between meeting people and performing, for every sale was a performance, troubled him.

Even though he had promised his wife to be careful about picking up hitchhikers, for terrible things happened these days, he usually ended up keeping his eyes peeled for figures by the side of the road. They almost always turned out to be college students or young men going in search of some adventure. He was reminded of himself and his youth in the drab days of the Depression.

By now it was almost dawn with the sky already gray and lightened. Lee Southgate's headlights leapt to discover and reveal a small shape, like a boy's, standing by the side of the road. Surprised, then relieved, he slowed down and stopped, opened the door.

When the man climbed in, a small man, almost a kind of dwarf, old and dirty, his right hand jammed in his pocket, and without a word, just climbed in, pulled the door to and looked straight ahead waiting to get going, Lee Southgate wished that he had passed by.

He just might have a knife in that pocket, Lee Southgate was thinking. *A crazy, twisted, little old man like that might do most anything.*

He drove on.

"Been waiting long?"

The man twisted to look at him, to look him over, scornful,

surprised, and maybe even outraged at being asked a question. He did not reply for a while. He waited so long to answer that Lee Southgate wondered if he had really heard him at all.

"Long enough," he said. "I like to have froze down to the bones waiting for you to get here."

"Well, well! Well, then. Let me just turn the heater on and see if we can't take the chill off."

The man grunted at that and looked away again, staring at the dark nothing out of the window. As if to say it would take more than a heater and a few kind, impersonal words to get rid of *his* chill. Lee Southgate stifled a belch. He was beginning to suffer from indigestion. He almost always did have indigestion after he had eaten without really being hungry and when he was very tired. A man could change all that, lose the slump of sheer fatigue and the growl in his stomach, once he found a motel, took himself a good hot shower, and changed his clothes.

Furtively he sized up his passenger. One thing was for sure, *he* hadn't been near a bath or a basin of water for quite a while. He had noticed his clothes in the quick, impersonal, complete manner of a salesman when the door opened for him to get in and the overhead light briefly bathed the car in a yellow glow. Now without even looking he could see the separate parts. The shoes, worn, run down flat at the heels, scuffed and paper-thin. The pants dirty, ragged, and stained. Then the strange thing was the jacket, an expensive one, suede, a genuine luxury item. It had looked to be fairly clean too and didn't come close to fitting him. The sleeve almost hid his thumb. Maybe somebody down the road had given it to him. Then again maybe he stole it. If he had a knife in his pocket he might have just taken it off somebody. It would be a big man too.

74

"Where are you headed, old-timer?"

"South, if it's anybody's business but my own."

"You don't say," Lee Southgate said, for the moment too pleased with the sound of another voice to care what was said.

"And another thing."

"What's that?"

"My name is not *old* timer."

"No offense meant," he said, smiling. "My name's Lee Southgate."

"Okay. Pleased to meet you. But just never mind who I am."

"Is it supposed to be a secret?"

"A *secret*? What do you mean making a crack like that?"

The old man turned again to stare at him with that same leathery crinkled expression of suspicion, curiosity, outrage, and incredulity. A mad look. Small as a boy or a jockey he was all right. Lee Southgate was drawn irresistibly, as to a kind of magnetic appeal, to think about that hidden right hand in its pocket. *Who knows? He might even have some kind of a little zip gun. Or maybe an old-fashioned set of brass knuckles. Most likely a knife though, one with an edge like a straight razor.*

He reached over and punched on the radio. If he wasn't going to be able to share a decent conversation, he could at least listen to something. They could listen together. That would be sharing *something*. Lee Southgate fiddled with the dial until he picked up, faint and static-clouded, an all-night disc-jockey show. He hummed along with the music and watched the road ahead swimming in the bright glare of his headlights. He felt better.

After a while he realized that his companion was still staring directly at him, waiting for something, maybe for the

75

answer to the question he'd asked that Lee Southgate had already forgotten. Lee Southgate looked quickly at him and flashed an amiable smile.

"It ain't a secret. You'd know it. You'd know it in a minute if I was to tell you."

"Is that a fact?" Lee Southgate began. Then, as if on second thought: "Sure now, I guess I would."

That seemed to satisfy the old man. He nodded solemnly, looked away, and eased back in the seat again. Lee Southgate shrugged and kept his mind on the driving. When the old man decided to speak again, it was so soft, almost a whisper against the noise of the radio, that Lee Southgate wasn't sure whether he had heard him say something or not.

"What's that? Excuse me, did you say something?"

"You could hear fine if it wasn't for that damn noise on the radio."

"Oh, I'm sorry." He twisted a knob on the radio and then the only noise was the slight whisper of the heater and its whirring fan.

"Thibault, I said. Battling Bill Thibault from New Orleans."

"Is that a fact?"

"Battling Bill Thibault, that's who I am."

There was a kind of patronizing smile about the way he said it though his fierce expression did not change.

"You don't say. What's your line of work, Mr. Thibault."

"My what?"

"Line of work. Occupation."

The old man gasped in simple amazement.

"*You don't know?* You mean to tell me that you ain't never *heard* of me? Where the hell have you been?"

"Excuse me," Lee Southgate started to say, "I'm sorry, but—"

"Where were you hiding when I took on Brakeman Shriver in Mobile? Didn't you even *hear* what I done to Burr Beaver in Houston, Texas? And you know damn well that Beaver, he went on to fight for the Championship of the World. You know they let that Burr Beaver have a shot at the Championship and I had already *proved* I was twice the man Beaver was."

So that's it! Just a punchy old prizefighter!

"That must have been a while ago, Mr. Thibault."

The old man giggled.

"Well, I guess so. I would say so. Likely you weren't even born yet, a young fellow like you."

"I guess that's why I never heard of you."

"That's no excuse. It isn't like I was just nobody. I was famous."

"Sure," Lee Southgate said, irritated. "You may be famous *yet* for all I know. I don't follow the fight game."

To Lee Southgate's surprise the old man winced away at that. He pressed his face flat against the glass of the rolled-up window.

"What's the use?"

It was a rhetorical question.

"Those were the days," the old man went on. "That was the time. It was the time of tall men. You won't believe it, but even me, a little old bird like me, I was a tall man in those days. It was good to be alive then. Nowadays there's nothing. This here is a bad time, the time of bitter children. There's not one man among you any more."

Then Lee Southgate was left with the heater to listen to and the road to watch and the sense that even though he had hurt the old man's feelings—and he was sensitive to other people's feelings and hated, usually, to hurt them—that he had accidentally saved himself from something bad, discomfort, trouble, some kind of real disaster. He *could* have been more polite with the old bum, feigned an interest anyway, but, obscurely threatened, he had told the truth. Lee Southgate was perplexed, baffled with himself. Why had he been compelled to offend the old man so?

It was early morning now. They had come out of the mountains of North Carolina and were in Tennessee, passing small farms and coming towards Johnson City. Lee Southgate's appointment was in Chattanooga, but he felt so tired he decided after all that he would stop off in Johnson City at least long enough to get a barbershop shave.

"How far did you say you were going, old-timer?"

"I didn't say. But I'm trying to get as far as Chattanooga."

"I'm stopping off in Johnson City. I'll let you off anywhere you want."

"I want to go to Chattanooga."

Here we go, Lee Southgate thought. *Here we go again*.

"Oh, you'll get a ride easy from here on."

"I'm sick and tired of having to get in and out of cars and trucks and standing by the road and waiting for rides to come along. All I want to do is get where I'm going."

"You ought to take the bus or the train."

The old man certainly brought out the worst in him. Maybe he was just tired out, worn beyond endurance, down to the bone marrow and the raw edges of his nerves. Truly he couldn't wait to get the old man out of the car and out of his sight.

As soon as they were in town, he pulled over and parked. People were already on the way to work, moving with purpose along the sidewalks to shops and offices. The mountains, the lonesome road, and the night seemed far behind. He felt much better.

78

"All right, Mr. Battling Bill Thibault, this is where you get off. End of the line."

Thibault, or whatever his name was, started to ease himself out of the car without a word.

"Why don't you take the bus from here on?"

No answer, but he stopped moving and waited.

"I'll tell you what," Lee Southgate said. "I'll give you enough money to have breakfast and buy yourself a bus ticket."

"What for? I ain't done nothing for you. What do I have to do for it?"

"Nothing."

"People don't give money for nothing."

Lee Southgate had an inspiration. Why not?

"Okay, I'll tell you what," he said. "I'll give you the money for your knife."

"What knife? I ain't got one. What do I need a knife for?"

"Show me what you're hiding in your right hand pocket and I'll give you the money."

The old man's rat-face wrinkled with curiosity. Thibault had to think about it.

"You gonna give me some money just to look at my bad hand?"

Delicately he slipped his hand out of his pocket and showed it to the salesman. It was puffed and swollen out of all shape and proportion, red as a cooked lobster and the skin stretched taut, terribly infected. Southgate looked and saw that it seemed to throb with each pulse beat. The old man looked at it too for a moment, but impersonally, as if it were a separate thing, maybe a small sick animal, no part of him.

Lee Southgate, sickened and ashamed, fumbled for a wad of dollar bills without counting them. The old man snatched them and, without a word, stepped out of the car.

Southgate started the car and drove away in a hurry, not willing to glance back. And so he never saw, would never even imagine the expression of simple childish pleasure and victory on the old man's face.

in the briar patch

Mother told Velma not to take us to the park anymore, but she *would* do it anyway.

"It's too hot for them to walk that far," Mother said, "and I want you to let them play around here."

"They likes to go," Velma said.

"I know that *you* like to go there and see your friends," Mother said, "but I don't want them to walk all that way in this hot weather."

"We just go along slow and takes our time," Velma said.

"I don't want them to go to the park."

"Yessm."

But sure enough she'd do it anyway. Just as soon as Mother got in the car, all dressed up to go somewhere, and smiled and waved at us with her gloves on, Velma would be planning to take us to the park. We all knew why she liked to go there and we didn't especially mind. Velma wanted to see Leroy. He wouldn't come to the house. He would wait for her in the park.

We'd go up the boulevard and we *did* take our time. That was because of little Johnny. He had to stop and look at everything even if he'd seen it a hundred times before. We had to walk on a certain side of the street to suit him. We'd go up one side and come back the other and if Velma forgot and took us on the wrong side little Johnny would start crying and kicking. He's only two. Mary, she's five now and right in the middle. She liked to go because they had swings and see-saws there, and besides Velma would get her dressed up like she was going to somebody's birthday or to Sunday School. Velma would fix her hair and put a little of her own perfume on Mary so she'd smell sweet to herself. All the other colored maids would say how pretty Mary looked today, and Mary liked that and so did Velma. The reason I went along was because Velma told me Leroy was a soldier.

The first time we ever saw Leroy, Velma walked all around the park with us, speaking to the other maids, laughing and joking with the young ones like herself and being sort of quiet and well behaved in front of the older ones. We did that too. When Velma was talking to the young ones we'd play around, chasing each other and splashing water in the fountain. But when Velma was talking to the older ones we'd be very polite. We'd hold hands and stand together like we were having our picture taken. We did that to make Velma feel better and so that she didn't have to worry about us. The first time we saw Leroy I knew that's what Velma had come to the park for, but Velma walked us all around the park before she noticed him. He was lying on a green bench in the shade with a newspaper over his face. Finally we stopped where he was and Velma pretended to be surprised to see him there. You'd be surprised how much pretending goes on.

"Why Leroy, what on earth brings you to the park?"

"I was just about to give up," he said. "I thought maybe you decided not to come."

He was a great big colored man, about twice as big as my father, and he had a long sad face like a cocker spaniel.

"Did you have to wait a long time?" Velma said. You could tell from the way that she asked it that she knew he'd been waiting a long time.

"As I recollect," he said, "you said something about two-thirty."

He looked close at his wrist watch. It was a wonderful big watch with a wide gold band.

"It's now close to four o'clock," he said.

"*Did* I say two-thirty?"

Velma started to laugh and so did Leroy for no reason at all and then he kissed her right in front of us.

"If he's a soldier, where's his uniform?" I asked Velma.

"Who said I was a soldier?" he asked. He sounded mad.

"Velma, you told me he was a soldier. He don't look like one to me."

"This here is Henry," Velma said, pointing to me. "He so smart. He notices everything. Henry likes soldiers a lot."

Leroy smiled all of a sudden and he shook hands with me.

"Well, Henry," he said, "I'm sure enough a soldier."

"But where's your uniform?"

Then he and Velma together explained to me that soldiers dress just like anybody else most of the time except when they're on the battlefield or in a parade. They sat down on the bench together while Mary had a swing and little Johnny played in the dirt. I stayed quiet and just looked because I had never seen a soldier up close before. My dad *used* to be a soldier in the war and Mother keeps a picture of him in his uniform on the bureau, but he explained to me that he wasn't the kind of soldier who shoots at people. He has an Army pistol anyway. It hangs by a strap from the head of his bed and we can't play with it. He keeps it in case somebody comes in the house at night because Mother is afraid of that. I found out that Leroy had shot plenty of people. He told me so himself.

I could see right away that Leroy was Velma's boy friend and I went and told Mary about it and told her to keep quiet about it. But she *would* ask Velma if what I said was right. Velma said yes, it was true, but it was a big secret and that we must help her keep it. We thought about it and Velma bought us all ice-cream cones at the drugstore so we said we would. Naturally little Johnny was too young and too dumb to know what we were talking about. But Velma bought him an ice-cream cone too. Just in case.

I don't know whether Mother knew about Leroy or not. I think she knew we were going to the park though because she would always remember to tell Velma not to take us there and once in a while she would ask me what we'd been doing all afternoon. I'd say we'd been playing and she'd say, where? I hated to tell her a lie but I knew it would get Velma in trouble if I told her the truth. I didn't want to get Velma in trouble. I was on Velma's side.

Mother never did like Velma much. Velma came to work for us after Lizzie got too old to ride the bus and climb the stairs anymore. Lizzie was nice and I liked her but she was different from Velma. When Lizzie got through cleaning up the house she would go sit at the kitchen table and read out of her Bible. She had a big reading glass and she couldn't read as well as I can. Sometimes she would have to get me to read to her and I was only in the second grade. Velma could read anything. She had lipstick on and she smoked cigarettes. She could work twice as fast as Lizzie and if nobody was around she'd go sit in the living room and smoke and drink coffee and read the paper or a magazine. She played the radio and she talked on the telephone. She was pretty and nice to us but she had her own way of doing things and Mother didn't like her. Right after Velma came to work for us Mother argued with Daddy about the cigarettes. I knew she didn't care about the cigarettes. She smokes herself sometimes. But she didn't like Velma and she knew Daddy didn't smoke.

"I can't see any harm in the girl having a smoke now and then if she wants one," he said, "as long as she does her work and doesn't burn the house down."

"Oh John," Mother said, "don't talk like that. She just *might* set the house on fire. You know how niggers are—so careless."

"Now, don't get excited," he said.

"No, I won't get excited. What difference does it make if I come home sometime and find the house in ruins and the children burned to a crisp?"

"Now, Lucille," he said, "be reasonable."

"That's it," Mother said, "be *reasonable,* be calm, don't *ever* get excited about anything! You just don't understand. You don't understand at all."

She looked like she might start to cry any minute so he went over and patted her.

"I understand," he said. "But let's give the girl a chance. She's new and she deserves a fair chance."

That's the way Mother and Daddy are. She has to get all upset and then he pays attention to her. Once I even saw her slap him in the face when they didn't know I was looking at them. They always make up though.

I wanted to get in good with Velma because she was new so I told her about the cigarettes. After that she would always empty the ash trays and wash them before Mother got home. And she wouldn't smoke at all if Mother was in the house. I heard Mother telling one of her friends she didn't know how long she was going to keep Velma. She said Velma was one of the new kind of maids—so uppity. I went and told Velma that too and Velma just laughed. I felt pretty bad about telling on Mother. I only did it to get in good with Velma.

Velma and Leroy liked each other a lot, you could tell. We used to go to the park every day that summer to see Leroy. I liked him too. He told me all about the Army and about war. He showed me a scar he had on his leg that he got in the war and he told me he had some others too but they had all healed up. He promised he would wear his uniform for me sometime but he never did. Sometimes he would bring his guitar along and play songs. He really could play the guitar. I liked the sound of it. You could make it sound sad or happy or make anything else you wanted if you only knew how to play on it like Leroy.

One time he brought a friend with him. His friend was fat and yellow-colored. He looked like a sleepy bullfrog. They had a bottle of whiskey and they were drinking out of it. This made Velma mad. She didn't say anything and she kept on smiling but I could feel that it made her mad at Leroy and she didn't like his friend. Leroy said he was going to come to our house and pick her up after work. He said he was tired of waiting on the bus every night. Velma told him not to.

"Why not?" he asked.

"Mister Duncan, he's a lawyer."

"What do I care about Mister Duncan? He ain't got nothing to do with me. I'll come right to the front door if I feel like it."

Leroy could get mad sometimes. I don't think he wanted Velma to work for us. He told her he'd be glad when she didn't have to do housework any more. She laughed at him and said if she counted on *him* she'd have to work the rest of her life. He was so lazy and good for nothing, Velma said.

"Just make sure you don't come around the Duncan's front door to pick me up that's all," she said. "Because if you do, I don't know you. I'm going to walk right past you."

"I bet you would," he said and his friend laughed.

"Leroy, he's just liable to have you slapped in the jail-house."

"Huh! I'd like to see the day."

"Well the day won't be long if you keep the kind of company you do, if you know what I mean."

Leroy and his friend laughed and we went home. Just the same Leroy didn't come around to pick up Velma. I liked Leroy all right but I was glad Daddy could have him slapped in jail if he wanted to. It made me feel better about Daddy. One time I asked Velma if Daddy could have her slapped in jail too.

"Now what would he want to do that for, Henry?" she laughed.

"I mean if he wanted to, could he?"

"Well, I guess he could," she said. "Your Daddy's a lawyer and I guess he could."

I wanted to ask him about it but I was afraid he'd find out about us going to the park if I did. He can find out almost any secret if he tries.

Just at the end of the summer Leroy and Velma had a fight. We stopped going to the park for about a week and I kept asking her when we were going to see Leroy again. She said she didn't know. Then one day we went. He was there all right, sitting on a bench, but Velma told us please not to pay any attention to him. We walked right past the bench he was sitting on. He jumped up and grabbed Velma.

"Where do you think *you're* going?" he said.

"I can't see that it's anybody's business but mine," she said.

"Oh you can't? You think you're so smart."

"I'm smart enough to know my friends when I see them."

"You're too smart for your own good."

"Take your hands off of me, Leroy, before I call a policeman."

"You *do* call a policeman," he said, "and it'll be the last thing you ever do."

"Oh you're a big tough guy, a big bad man. I know a thing or two."

"Well, you better keep what you know to yourself."

"I will if it suits me."

He started to call her names. She told him to hush his mouth in front of the children. He said they weren't *his* children. That made Velma start to cry. He told her to please stop crying before somebody saw her.

"That's all *you* care about," she said. "You don't care about the *cause* of it. All you want to do is to keep out of trouble."

She said she hoped he ended up in jail. He said if he did he would sure know who to thank for it. She said he'd better be careful. Then Leroy slapped her face hard. He said he would make her awful sorry if she did anything about it and then he walked away out of the park and up the street without even looking back.

Everybody was crying except me. Velma was crying and Mary was crying and that made little Johnny cry too. We started home on the wrong side and then he *really* started to cry.

"What's the matter with you, little boy?" Velma said. "Stop crying, Johnny. Please stop crying. Velma's going to buy you an ice-cream cone."

"We're walking home the wrong way," I said.

"Oh," Velma said. "In my haste I forgot all about that."

So we crossed over and everything was all right. I didn't say anything for a while. I wanted to wait until everybody had finished crying. When they did I asked Velma what Leroy didn't want her to tell.

"Never mind about that," she said.

"Well, are you *going* to tell?"

"I don't know what to do," she said. "I just don't know."

That night Mother and Daddy went to the picture show. Velma put little Johnny to bed right after his supper and a little later she put Mary to bed too. I was playing with my soldiers in my room but she wanted me to come play in the living room.

"Why?"

"I want to sit in there by the radio."

"Well, you go listen to the radio and I'll play in here."

"No," she said. "You can bring the soldiers to the living room."

So I took them in there and spread them out on the rug while she sat in a chair by the radio and smoked. Every once in a while she would get up and make sure the doors were all locked. It was getting late and I was getting sleepy. After a while the doorbell started ringing.

"Who is it? Who's there?" she called.

There wasn't any answer. She got up from the chair and cocked her head to listen. She looked scared.

"What's the matter with you, Velma?" I asked.

It made me feel scared too. She just stood there listening. After a minute the doorbell started ringing again and it kept on ringing. She took me by the hand.

"Come on, Henry," she said. "Let's us go answer the door."

She held on to me tight.

"Is it Leroy?" I asked.

"No. He wouldn't dare come right to the front door and ring the bell. It must be somebody else."

She opened the door a little bit to look out. It *was* Leroy and he pushed in the door. He was dirty and sweaty and panting.

"Get out of this house," she said. "Can't you see I've got this child here with me?"

"You knew it all the time," he said. "When you came to the park this afternoon you already had done called the police."

"Never mind about that," Velma said. "You better get out of here quick before Mister Duncan comes in. He going to be here any minute and if he catch you in the house he's going to kill you."

"He's sure going to be surprised at what he finds when he gets home," Leroy said.

She turned me loose and tried to run for the kitchen. He caught her and hit her with his fist and then they started fighting. She was yelling and fighting back and crying all at the same time. They fought in the living room and knocked over the radio. Leroy was stepping all over my soldiers on the rug but I was so excited I didn't even think of crying. Velma started having a nosebleed and she fell down but he kept on hitting her and kicking her. She just rolled up in a ball on the floor. About that time Daddy came running in the front door. He still had the car keys in his hand when he ran in the living room.

"What the hell is going on?" he said.

Leroy turned around quick and hit Daddy and started running for the back of the house. Daddy ran up the stairs and got his Army pistol. I heard him shooting it off the up-stairs back porch. Then he came down with the gun in his hand. He told Velma to go in the back bathroom and get cleaned up. He told me to get to bed, but I hid in the hall upstairs where I could hear what was going on. He called the police. He was talking on the phone when Mother came in. She took one look and started crying right away.

90

"I told you something like this would happen," she said.

"Never mind what you told me," he said. "Go up and see if the children are all right."

"You don't have to wave that pistol at me," she said.

By the time she got upstairs I was in my bed with my eyes closed. She looked around in all the bedrooms and saw that everything was all right. Mary and little Johnny had slept right through all of it. Then she went in the bathroom and left the door open. I could see her putting some lipstick on and powdering her face. She went downstairs again and I slipped back into the hall.

"This nigger got her pregnant," Daddy said to her, "and he wouldn't marry her. He's AWOL from the Army so she told the police where he was living."

"I told you that girl was no good," Mother said. "He could have killed you. She brought nothing but trouble."

"Well," he said, "I promise you, you won't have to worry about it any more."

He went in the kitchen and got them both a drink and they sat down in the living room. I could hear Velma crying in the kitchen. After a while a police car came and they had Leroy. They brought him to the front door and I leaned over the banister to watch. He looked funny under the porch light. I could see he was scared but he was acting scareder than he really was and he was bent over trying to look small.

"Is this the nigger?" one of the policemen asked.

"It sure looks like it," Daddy said. "But they all look alike."

"Go get Velma," he told Mother.

Velma was crying and hiding her face. She didn't want to look at Leroy but they made her and she said yes it was him. My Dad stood right in front of him for a minute looking at him. They looked about the same size because Daddy was standing up straight trying to look tall and Leroy was trying to look small. Then Daddy hit him in the face with the pistol.

Leroy started crying and moaning and saying he didn't mean to do it and he was sorry. He said they could do what they wanted with him but *please* don't give him back to the Army. The policemen had a hold of him and all of a sudden it reminded me of the story Lizzie used to tell me about Br'er Rabbit and the Tarbaby. I liked that story and I thought the rabbit was awful smart to pretend he didn't want to get thrown in the briar patch. The policemen laughed and one of them said that's exactly what was going to happen to Leroy. They were so dumb. I don't see how they couldn't catch on that he was pretending.

Daddy told the policemen to take Leroy away from the house. Velma started crying louder. She yelled at Leroy that she was sorry she had got him into all this. Daddy told her she might as well get her pocketbook and go on home. He told her not to come back. He gave her some money but he didn't even count it. He just handed it to her. I ran up to the front bedroom window to wave back at her if she waved to me. But she didn't look back. She just walked out on the sidewalk hanging her head and looking all loose-jointed like a doll. She looked sad under the streetlight waiting for the bus to come.

I sneaked back to my room and listened. Mother and Daddy came up the stairs together. Mother was laughing.

"You surprised me, John."

"Don't play with that," he said. "It's loaded."

"I didn't know you had it in you."

"There's lots of things you don't know," he said. "Here, give me the pistol."

He sounded tired. She laughed and whispered something I couldn't hear to him. Then she went in the bathroom and I could hear her brushing her teeth. Daddy was outside my door for a minute. I could hear him breathing hard the way Lizzie used to after she climbed the stairs. Then he came in my room and looked down at me without turning the light on. I kept my face next to the pillow so I could look at him with one eye without him knowing that I was awake. He had the pistol in his hand but he was holding on to it loose. I thought he was going to drop it on the floor. He looked tired and loose-jointed just like Velma, and I was afraid he might fall on the floor too. I knew he couldn't be pretending because he thought I was asleep. I couldn't see whether he was crying or not. I wanted to get out of bed and tell him I felt the same way he did so he would feel better. But I knew he'd be mad that I wasn't asleep when he thought I was. After a while he walked down the hall and looked at Mary and little Johnny. Then he went in his room. I could hear Mother still brushing her teeth. No wonder they stayed so white. That reminded me I hadn't brushed mine. I decided I might as well wait until in the morning as long as nobody knew the difference.

LION

In the morning they came back, two of them anyway, just
as he knew they would.

With the first gray hints of light, when all the earth's as
ghostly as a moon and the smell of a new day is as keen and
sweet as mint, Jojo was up out of bed and stealthily crept to
the window. Quick as a monkey he jumped from the window
sill across the breathless space to catch, in his fall, the limber
branch of the oak tree that grew nearest to the house. For
an instant, waiting for his breath to come again, letting his
heart fall back into its place, he hung on to the limb trembling from the shock, then swung high and easy, skinning the
cat until he was safely on the limb. The rest was simple. He
straddled the limb and slid down. Where it joined the trunk

94

he swung free once again and dropped lightly to the ground. Then he heard the roosters start to crow all over town.

The rest of them, his family, would still be sound asleep. And at breakfast time who would miss *him* with so much going on, Raymond and Stony and Daddy all yelling for their breakfast at the same time in one loud voice, all of them going to be late for work; Marcia lingering ("loitering" Sue calls it) in the bathroom, taking her sweet time while Sue stands just outside the door, leaning thin and weary against it, beating on it and yelling bloody murder about what *difference* does it make how a *telephone operator* looks, she, Sue, being the receptionist for Doctor Trout the chiropractor, has got to look pretty; and Marcia shouting back at her in her bright voice, cruel as a new knife, that Sue can spend all day and all night too in the bathroom if she wants to and she'll never look pretty to anybody; then come the tears and more loud beating on the door, and Marcia flushes the pot so she won't have to listen; while down in the kitchen Mama and Dalmatia, the colored maid, both of them huge and identically awkward as a couple of trained bears dancing on their hind legs, both so alike they might as well be the same person in two different shades like dolls, both sleepy-eyed, both sloppy, stumbling and blundering into each other and nodding their *excuse-me-please's* as the bacon and eggs and toast burn to a crisp and the coffee boils over on the stove; neither of them will speak a word to anyone or to each other until the others have all spilled out of the front door in a simultaneous rush to leave, such a rush to the sidewalk they must seem like a handful of pennies hurled from the house; then the two of them will sit down at the kitchen table, enormous, bulging over their chairs on both sides, and over their own coffee will at last come to life, begin to talk and laugh together; in the midst of all that, who'd even notice

95

the presence or absence of Jojo, figuring him small and safe at school or somewhere, even though it's midsummer already and school's been out a long time; he whom his mother calls, always with a great laugh, her little P.S.?

So Jojo slipped away, quick and quiet as a shadow, and went downtown.

There, just as he had known, there were two of them anyway, sitting in the beat-up clay- and mud- and dust-covered ghost of a car with the cross-eyed headlights, parked directly in front of the Sheriff's brick, one-story office. The one behind the wheel was bald as a rock and short too, pretty nearly some kind of a midget or a dwarf, wearing a sweat-soaked white shirt with the sleeves rolled up to the shoulder around arms like sausages, mopping at his bald head with a handkerchief gray as a dust rag, peering out at the empty street through glasses as thick as the bottom of a pop bottle behind which his large pale eyes glistened and swam like fish in a bowl.

"Jesus, Jesus," he kept saying. "We drive half the night to get here and then the bastard's still asleep."

The other grunted and stayed where he was, hunched over on the other side of the front seat with his face pressed against the rolled-up window glass. He was thin-faced as a hawk and very dark, and his black hair shone so and was cut so neat you wouldn't believe it could be real. He had a little mustache the same way, thin and straight like it was painted on, and the eyebrows too, so black, so trim, so emphatic, they weren't to be believed. His eyes were weary and bored and unseeing like the little glass eyes of a doll. His lips, to Jojo's surprise, looked painted on with lipstick. He wore a dark coat and a bright shirt and a yellow necktie pulled all the way to the top just like it wasn't summer, and he didn't seem to be sweating at all. He could do whatever he

96

pleased. He was Alonzo the Lion Tamer. Jojo knew his face, the tired blind eyes, red lips, slick black hair, from the yellow posters and from what had happened last evening as well. The other one was the owner or the manager, whoever is the boss of The Grand Clark Brothers' Travelling Circus.

While Jojo stood staring, the Lion Tamer rolled down the window on his side and extended, lazy, his hand with a coin in it.

"Little boy," he said. "Run and get us some coffee."

Jojo snatched the fifty-cent piece from that pale cool palm, cool as a flower, and he started running up the sidewalk to the French Cafe, hearing over his shoulder the other one saying "Jesus, you'd think he'd be here waiting for us at a time like this."

Last evening at dusk, just on the shores of darkness, with the last of the sun like a great splash of blood on the sky and already the first stars floating in the waning blue like lights reflected in water, Jojo had seen how it all happened. It began when out of nowhere, as if by magic, first came the car, the same one with the cross-eyed headlights, then the big trucks, so worn and dusty, so solemn and slow in line they seemed like a parade of shambling prehistoric beasts out of a picture book, blindly following one behind the other. And he knew at once because of the yellow posters which had popped up brightly on walls and telephone poles a week or so before that this had to be The Grand Clark Brothers' Travelling Circus. He knew, too, from listening around to what everybody said when the posters first appeared, that the circus would not be stopping *here*, only passing through on the way to the city. He left one of his secret hiding places, one of his tree places where he could see everything that went on and not be seen, and he followed after, joined the wild herd of children, black and white, and, it seemed, all the yapping mongrel dogs in creation, wishing as he ran along that he was a little bit older, that like the big high-school boys he could have his own bike to join in the procession, to wheel precariously, dangerously in and out of the coughing, ambling trucks, shouting, shrill as birds, and with sometimes no hands at all on the handle bars.

He followed them all the way through town and to the place just beyond the last of the houses where they pulled off the road and parked in a line. The Bald Man was there then, running up and down the line of trucks, shouting at the drivers, pointing, waving his hands, and always only shrugging when any of them leaned out of the high cabs to ask him a question. Jojo wandered under and around the trucks, smelling all the strangeness, staring at the people who climbed out stiff-legged, stretching, to look with indifferent eyes at the town they had just passed through and the darkening land. The Bald Man got one of them to open a fire hydrant, the last one in town, placed out there in the field in a dream of expansion, and the men came with buckets. It didn't take long, either, for the Fire Chief in his red car and the Sheriff in his black one to come too. They came whizzing, sirens whining, and walked ponderously over and began to yell at the Bald Man above the noise of the running water and the catcalls of the men carrying buckets to and fro. They yelled, both at once, at the Bald Man, and he in turned yelled back at them, waved his little arms, shrugged, and mopped his brow. By the time Jojo got there to stand close by with the rest of the children, they had stopped shouting, though they were still talking.

"We got to have some water for the animals," the Bald Man said. "That's all I'm asking for. Just a little water."

"Seems to me you might have asked first," the Sheriff said, putting his hands inside the black leather belt that creaked with the bulk of him, that winked with a row of shiny bullets and from which, sacrosanct, his pearl-handled revolver sagged in its polished holster.

"We didn't think you folks would begrudge us a little water."

"You're supposed to get permission," the Fire Chief said. "You got to have permission first."

"How long do you plan to be here?" the Sheriff said.

"Just a little while, captain," the Bald Man said. "It won't take long."

"Make sure it don't."

Jojo left them all standing around the fire hydrant where the water flowed and spread on the ground and the men with buckets came and went, slipping and staggering in the fresh mud. He ignored the people who had come out of the trucks and huddled together in groups nearby. None of them were freaks or had costumes on anyway. He sneaked among the trucks, sniffing for dry hay and the dungy, rich odor of animals, wishing that there was some way he could get to see them. He could smell them in some of the trucks, hear them moving about inside, but it was going to be hard to get a real look at them. He came to the end of the line.

Disappointed then, waiting for a sign or a glimpse of something strange, hiding under the last truck in the line, leaning against a pair of perfectly smooth tires taller than he was, he saw and recognized at once from the posters Alonzo the Lion Tamer. He came and stood so close that Jojo could have reached out and touched him. He leaned back against the side of the truck. He was wearing riding britches and a high-necked sweater, and he was smoking a little cigar. But Jojo smelled above the familiar odor of leather boots and a cigar something sweet like roses, like Sue's perfume.

A woman in a red T-shirt and red trousers so tight around

her legs and hips they looked to have been painted on her came there and talked to the Lion Tamer in a low voice.

"You smell like a French cat-house," she said and her teeth showed very white in the increasing darkness.

"You ought to know," he said. "I wouldn't."

"Can't you take a joke? Can't you tell when I'm joking?"

"Sure," he said. "You got some rich sense of humor. You slay me."

"What's the *matter* with you? What is your wife supposed to do, draw pictures for you?"

"That I'd like to see. I'd like to see the kind of pictures you'd draw."

"You should hear what the others say about you."

"Who cares about them? What do they know, anyway?"

"Isn't it a big laugh?"

"Here we go again," he said. "More jokes."

"For the first time in my life I'm with a man I could really like and he turns out to be a cheap ungrateful bastard."

"*Like?*" the Lion Tamer said. "Who wants *like?*"

"You can't really *love* somebody unless they will give you half a chance."

"You don't know anything about love. Nobody knows anything about love. It's a mystery."

The Lion Tamer cleared his throat and spat on the ground by his boots.

"I guess it just serves me right," she said.

"Truth," he said. "You want to know the truth. Sometimes you make me sick. You make me so sick I could puke."

He threw his cigar away and turned his back on her, stalking up the line of trucks in giant steps, his high boots squeaking, the faint sweet odor receding with him.

She remained where she was, her hands pressed over her face and her body shaking all over. When she took her hands away, Jojo could see that she was crying silently, and the tears seemed to cause the features of her face to melt and soften like hot wax. She smelled like soap. She slumped over and looked much older than at first. Jojo heard the men up ahead begin shouting and he listened to their calls being passed back along the line and to the engines of the trucks as they, one by one, began to growl. He wondered if he'd better move out from under the truck and let her see that he had been there the whole time, but before he could decide what he ought to do she moved. She straightened up, posed tensely, looking left and right like somebody getting ready to dash across a busy street, then she ran around behind the truck. He heard her fumbling with what must be a heavy chain. He heard the door open on rusty hinges.

First there was a strange odor, an animal smell for sure, but like wild dry grass and dust and dung. Then the lion came swiftly out on soft feet. He stood by the truck, great-maned, big-chested, head up high, sniffing the air. Jojo watched the lion go running off into the dark across the field and disappear. He heard the woman shut the door, trouble with the chain, and then she came walking right past him, smelling now of heavy sickly sweat like somebody with a fever, and breathing deep and hard as if she had been running a long way. Next, all the lights of the trucks came on at once, and as they started to move forward he jumped out of the way. He saw the huge tires roll over his footprints, and he stared after as the bright parade of vehicles picked up speed and vanished down the highway.

When the last red taillights were swallowed by the dark, he ran across the field, sniffing as he went, following the way the lion had gone.

When Jojo came back with two paper cups of hot coffee the

Sheriff was there, his black car parked at a jaunty angle, the way *he* was allowed to do, and the three of them were standing on the sidewalk. The Sheriff had his hands under his belt again and he was grinning.

"What is all this about anyway?" the Sheriff said. "What are you two trying to prove?"

"I told you on the phone," the Bald Man said. "Jesus, I thought you'd have a big bunch of men here to help us find him."

"I *had* one little talk with you yesterday evening," the Sheriff said. "Maybe you didn't quite get the point."

"Ask him," the Bald Man said pointing to the Lion Tamer. "See what he says."

Though the Lion Tamer was standing with them, he was aloof, not really looking at either of them. Now that the Lion Tamer was out of the car Jojo could see that he was wearing the same trim riding britches and high glossy boots. He also had yellow gloves on and carried a short riding crop. He still looked tired, weary and indifferent beyond telling, but in the plain daylight his color, his slick black hair, his razored mustache, his painted lips made him look like an undertaker's corpse. In fact he looked exactly the way he did on the posters, curiously two-dimensional. There was about him the faint sweetness of the night before. He simply stood there, gripping the riding crop behind his back with both gloved hands and looking through the two of them and the whole town too as if everything in the world had been made out of cellophane and as if, like some funnybook character with superhuman powers, he could see through everything under the sun.

"I wouldn't ask him anything," the Sheriff said. "I wouldn't ask *that* one the time of day."

"All right," the Bald Man said. "All right now. Let's don't

everybody get excited. Let's try and keep our wits about us."

He dabbed at the sweat on his shiny head, his jowled face and his neck. He was sweating so much that his white shirt stuck to him. His upper body was big as a barrel, but his legs were terribly thin and short, and Jojo was amazed at how small his feet were, tiny points in yellow and black shoes, just like a little girl's. On such delicate legs he looked something like a robin.

"Here, boy," the Lion Tamer said. And he took the cups of coffee and the three dimes change.

"You can have mine," the Bald Man said to the Sheriff. "I don't think I can keep it down now."

"Keep it," the Sheriff said. "I've had my breakfast."

So the two of them drank their coffee and the Sheriff watched them. When they finished the Lion Tamer lit up one of his little cigars and Jojo took the empty cups and put them in a trash can.

"Here's the way I look at it," the Sheriff said. "You claim you lost a lion last evening when you stopped here. You say you must have lost it then, but you don't know how—"

"I got a good idea how," the Lion Tamer said.

The Sheriff glared at him.

"We'll have plenty of time for your good ideas later."

"Okay," the Lion Tamer said. "Okay."

"Now take it easy," the Bald Man said.

"I said okay, didn't I?"

"Anyhow," the Sheriff said. "You want me to round up a whole bunch of men and hunt for this lion for you."

"Not just for us," the Bald Man said. "You don't want a wild beast prowling around town either."

The Sheriff just smiled.

"I want King back," the Lion Tamer said. "Give me a little help and I'll get him."

"King, that's his name?" the Sheriff said, giggling now.

The Lion Tamer flicked the ash off his cigar.

"That's logical," he said. "I call him King, so his name must be King."

"Don't you sass me, boy."

"Everybody calm down now," the Bald Man said, wringing out his handkerchief.

"All right," the Sheriff said. "There's just two ways to look at this situation. Either you lost a lion or you didn't. Now my suspicion is you didn't lose no lion here. It don't figure. So, if you're trying some kind of a publicity stunt . . ."

"Publicity stunt!" the Bald Man said. "Jesus! You got to believe us, man."

At that the Lion Tamer only smiled, showing his bright perfect teeth.

"If you are trying a stunt, I'll lock you both up," the Sheriff said. "I told you once to keep moving on and I meant it. We don't want no fly-by-night two-bit carnie around here. Period. Now let's look at it the other way. Suppose it's for real. Then it strikes me you folks are getting mighty careless with your wild animals."

"The bitch did it," the Lion Tamer said. "She don't care for King."

"That's against the law too," the Sheriff said, "turning lions loose and such. I could lock you up for that too."

"I don't know how it happened," the Bald Man said. "We got steel doors on those trucks and chains."

"Tell you what I'll do," the Sheriff said. "When the Deputy shows up, we'll take a little drive around and see what we can see. We'll take a look."

"We *got* to find him," the Bald Man said. "What if we don't find him?"

"Well, if he *is* here," the Sheriff said, "it looks like we got us the beginnings of a pretty good zoo."

"You could never keep King in no hick zoo," the Lion Tamer said.

After a while the Deputy came. The Sheriff went inside his office and got a rifle and a length of rope, and the Lion Tamer exchanged his riding crop for a big whip and buckled on his pistol belt. The four of them climbed into the Sheriff's car, the two from the circus sitting in the back. Just as they were pulling away the Lion Tamer rolled down the window and threw Jojo a dime. It rang like a little bell on the sidewalk.

"Thanks, boy."

Jojo pocketed the dime and walked around to the side of the office where the first shade was forming a pool and squatted, leaning his back against the brick wall. To be a Lion Tamer would be very, very special. You likely had to have a call for it like preaching. He closed his eyes to be able to picture how it would be, Alonzo the Lion Tamer caught in a net of golden lights, alone in a cage with all those lions and tigers while outside all around the hushed dark tent every burning eye would be fixed on him. That would be a lonely wonderful thing to be there in a bright fancy costume and prove to the world that one man all by himself can crack a whip and make even the wildest animals dance and stand as still as statues or jump through flaming hoops. Talk about jubilation! *Then* they would have to notice you and love you for what you proved to them could be done, how brave somebody could be. But it would be kind of sad too. How could you ever tell anybody how it was? What could you ever say to them after you came out of the terrible cage and bowed to them and they clapped for you? "It's only some kind of a trick," they would say. No wonder you would be so tired of everything.

And picturing all this Jojo dozed in the shade waiting for them to come back.

Maybe an hour or so passed, and then the Sheriff's car returned, cruising slowly up the street which was lively now with the morning's first business. The rifle was poking through the right front window where the Deputy cradled it. They all got out of the car and stood on the sidewalk.

"I'll give you two rare birds about twenty minutes to be outside of the county," the Sheriff said.

"Listen," the Bald Man said. "You got to warn people to be on the lookout—"

"Man, are you crazy? We got people worked up enough already wondering what we're doing driving around town with a loaded rifle in the morning," the Deputy said.

"Time's wasting," the Sheriff said, looking at his watch.

"All right, all right," the Bald Man said. "We're going."

The Lion Tamer spat on the sidewalk.

"Be careful," he said. "That King's a mean one."

Then for all the world to see he started crying right there on the sidewalk like a child. The Bald Man took his arm and led him to the cross-eyed car.

"Wait a minute," the Sheriff said. "Just in case we *do* find him, what does he like to eat?"

"Meat. Raw meat," the Lion Tamer said, still sobbing.

The Sheriff and the Deputy laughed as the beat-up crazy car made a big U-turn and disappeared swiftly the way it had come.

"Don't that beat the world?" the Deputy said.

"You know how come that fellow there wears perfume?"

"No. Not unless he's queer or something."

"I'll tell you," the Sheriff said. "It's because he's really a nigger. He may look like a white man, but I can tell every time. Let him try and hide the smell. You can always tell by the hair."

They both laughed as they strolled up the walk to the office.

106

That evening, just as he knew it would, all hell broke loose at home. There they were, all sitting around the dining room table, Raymond and Stony and Daddy, tired out from a hard day's work, banging their silverware on their empty plates and hollering for supper. His Mama and Dalmatia were staggering around the kitchen (they'd been drinking whiskey together, Jojo could smell that) looking everywhere for the missing steak.

"Come on," Raymond was yelling. "I ain't got all night."

Then his mama came as far as the kitchen door but not too close to the table. She leaned back against the door frame and smiled a little smile.

"We had a steak," she said. "But it's gone now. I mean we really had one, but I don't know what came of it."

"No *meat?*" Stony cried.

She shook her head slowly, still smiling.

"Great God Almighty!" his daddy shouted. "Come on, boys. Let's us go down to the French Cafe and get something to eat."

They shoved back their chairs and all at the same time threw their china plates against the wall, his mama's pretty white china ones, and the plates shattered beautifully in many pieces and fell like a noisy kind of snow on the floor. As the three men stomped out of the room his mama started to cry and Dalmatia came from the kitchen and put her arm around her. Jojo got down from his chair and tiptoed up-stairs. It was pretty bad up there, too, with Sue, a big pair of scissors in her hand, chasing Marcia around, both of them running up and down the hall as loud as runaway horses and in and out of all the rooms. Sue had only her slip on and Marcia wasn't wearing stitch one. Jojo stood in the hall and they ran all around him, as if he was a post or something. Sometimes you'd think the people didn't know he was alive around there. Then Jojo saw the water slowly spreading into the hall from under the bathroom door. The tub was over-flowing. He went into the bathroom—the door was on one hinge like a broken arm because Sue had knocked it open—and turned off the water and pulled the plug. Just outside the open door Marcia and Sue stopped running and, panting, glared at each other.

"Oh, Miss Priss," Sue said. "Trying to play innocent!"

"I haven't the slightest idea—"

"For once I'm the one with a date in the middle of the week and what do you do? You're so green-eyed with jealousy, you up and take my perfume."

"Hah!" Marcia said. "I wouldn't *use* your stinking perfume. And don't you act so holier than thou. Where's my new lipstick?"

"I'm sure I wouldn't know."

They continued to stare into each other's eyes, then Sue slapped Marcia, and Marcia unblinking slapped her back, and Sue dropped the scissors and went running back to her room crying, and she slammed the door so hard the whole house shook. Marcia whirled, smiling, and came into the bathroom.

"Oh," she said. "Oh, it's just you. Shut the door behind you. I'm trying to take a bath."

Jojo tiptoed to his room, shut the door, and lay on the bed with his eyes closed waiting for the dark to come.

As soon as it was good and dark, the stars all out and the subtle odors of the evening and the soft noises of insects rich and mysterious in the air, Jojo stirred. He rummaged in a great pile of his dirty clothes in the closet until he found his Canadian Royal Mounted Police costume that he got for last Christmas. It was already getting too tight, but he managed to get into it, though he couldn't button the scarlet jacket all the way down. He reached under his mattress and found the paper sack all right. He threw it out of the window. Then he hopped up on the window sill and squinted into the dark. Though he had done it so many times, in the dark it was always hard to see the limb. There was always one rushing moment when he couldn't be sure that he had judged the distance right. He crouched and jumped into the vacant air, holding his breath, his heart pounding until he felt the rough curve of the limb under his hands and he shivered from the shock. He climbed down the tree and picked up his bundle.

A good mile away, at the edge of town, there was a curious three-story frame house. It had belonged to a banker who shot himself when the Boom ended, and an old woman, his widow, crazy as a bat everyone said, lived there all alone. And it sagged from the careless weight of her loneliness and misery. The front yard, the front porch, were covered with junk—old shoes, umbrellas, newspapers, faded hats, broken toys, magazines, tires and inner tubes, even garbage; for that was all that she did for herself now. Late at night she would leave her lightless house and prowl the town, search-ing in trash heaps and garbage cans, poking among the smouldering things at the dump, searching for something, dragging a child's red wagon behind her until it was heaped, loaded with the wrecked, the broken, the thrown-away, for-saken things of the town. What these actions meant, nobody pretended to know. They left her to herself. After all her husband had been a respectable man in those years before the Depression, and who could blame her now, seeing she did no real harm?

Jojo circled around the house to the back yard, picking the way through the litter and wreckage of a garden. The smell of it was terrible to him, but no one lived near enough to complain, and the dogs loved it. Back farther there was a ramshackle barn, left over from the horse and buggy days.

Outside of this barn he stopped and opened the paper bag. He anointed himself with Sue's perfume. He painted his lips with Marcia's lipstick, then, carrying the paper sack with him, he pulled back the bolt on the door, cracked it, and slipped inside. It was dark and foul in the barn, but he could smell that the lion was still in there all right. There had always been the chance that someone, even the old woman herself, might find out before now. He was glad they hadn't.

Then he could see the eyes in the dark. They seemed green and glowing from an inner light like jewels. He opened the bag and took out the steak. Holding it in front of him, he began to walk slowly toward the burning eyes.

thus the early gods

"Decent people just don't act like that," her mother-in-law said.

Jane's mother-in-law was Mrs. Grim. How aptly named! Jane was amused by the thought until she reminded herself that it was her name too.

Jane's husband mumbled assent and held up his highball glass and looked through it to change the sky from blue to amber. Lately everything was being so changed.

Jane herself wasn't paying much attention to Mrs. Grim's desultory monologue. She sat with the other two on the front porch and looked on beyond the path that crawled like a lazy snake from the cottage through the dunes to the beach, beyond the glare and dance of light on the white sand of the beach and beyond the flourish of the breaking waves, perfectly ironed creases that became immaculate explosions into the dizzying blue of the sky, cloudless and pure today. There was a line of pelicans, a slightly lopsided V with one arm stretched out longer than the other, and they flew by with a brown sturdy grace like a crew of oarsmen in a racing shell. They followed the leader at the point. He (she guessed it would *have* to be a male) would spread his wings to soar, and all soared likewise, rising and hovering with delicate balance on invisible currents of air, maintaining always the shape and direction of the formation though, like a single, trained, instantaneous muscular action, like part of a dance. When he pumped his wide wings with a smooth strong motion, the others followed in quick succession. She liked to see them fishing and alone: the twisty, angled high dive followed by a small flash of white, and then up bobbed the pelican to float contented a while before flying again. She had seen them up close too, perched like silly newel posts on the pilings near the Fish Market, long-beaked, drab-feathered, clowns. And she had been disappointed. They seemed grotesquely comic. But now as formations of them passed by the front porch, at home in their native element of air, they seemed to be made of it, to partake of all the wild, wide-flung, dazzling substance and mystery and marvel of the sky. They were creatures of skill and grace and beauty, and she wished she could paint them.

But, of course, her paints were still packed tight in the wooden box underneath the double bed. She wouldn't dream of bringing them out.

"But they're so beautiful!" she exclaimed.

"*Who*?" the gray-haired woman, firmly in the rocking chair beside her, asked. "Who? Those Quiglys?"

"No, no," Jane said, laughing. "I was thinking about the pelicans."

Her mother-in-law snorted.

"I was speaking of the Quiglys."

Harper, Jane's husband, merely chuckled and sipped his drink.

Mrs. Grim had been talking about the Quigly family steadily ever since they had arrived and opened the beach cottage a few days (how many has it been already?) before. She noticed right away that they had been using her outside shower. ("Lord knows what kind of a staggering water bill I'll have!") She observed that they let their children run wild and free and naked as four little jaybirds all over the dunes and on the beach. And she complained that all of them, the gaunt, grinning scarecrow of a father included, used her path to the beach as if they had a perfect right to, instead of going the longer way around to the public approach. It was clear, too, at the outset that they had no pride.

The Grims hadn't been in the cottage five minutes before the man was standing at the back door, beating on it with bony knuckles, grinning and asking if he could borrow a quarter pound of butter and an electric iron, not explaining why, or, indeed, even making some kind of mannerable small talk about the casual incongruity of the two requests. He didn't introduce himself. He didn't bother to ask who they might be. He just asked for butter and the iron and then stood there waiting until he was given what he wanted.

Mrs. Grim had been fuming about the Quiglys ever since.

"Oh, Mother," Jane had said, mildly amused at first. "What's wrong with them? I mean really. They seem pleasant enough."

Her mother-in-law had stiffened.

"You're not from these parts," she had answered flatly. "So

113

you wouldn't be expected to know or make *distinctions*. They're trash, honey, that's all. Trash, pure and simple."

The element that added insult to injury for Mrs. Grim was the occupation of Joe Quigly, whom she insisted on calling The Man, never by name. It turned out that he was a bulldozer operator. Farther south, more than a mile down the beach, he was daily engaged in levelling the pristine dunes for something or other. A new subdivision of crackerbox houses maybe. Perhaps even a motel. She wouldn't condescend to inquire.

"It really shouldn't bother you," Jane had said. "There's so much space down there, and there's a whole mile between here and there."

"When we first built this place, my late husband and I," Mrs. Grim had told her, "there wasn't another cottage for miles. It was so peaceful. Now houses are popping up everywhere like the heat rash. Like pimples. They're tearing the dunes down, and new people—not the kind of people you'd care to have around if you had any say so about the matter— are coming here by the hordes to live. They're ruining the place. They're like a lot of weeds choking us out."

"You'd have to know how everything was in the beginning to appreciate what I mean," she added.

Of course, she never failed to remind Jane that she was an outsider, from the north, and wouldn't be expected to offer her opinions on subjects she couldn't possibly know anything about, among them the Quiglys. Jane never failed to resent this either.

At first, their very first night in the cottage, Harper, too, had been amused.

"Oh, you'll come to love her when you know her and understand her better," he said. "Everyone does. It's just that she was born out of her time or, anyway, that she had to live on beyond it. She's a lady living in a time when that word

114

doesn't mean anything. And all she sees around her is change, change, change. Change and decay. The good, happy, comfortable world she grew up in turned inside out, turned into something else after the Depression and the War. She's just a minor, eccentric victim of the great social revolution. A bewildered mastadon wandering around in the postglacial age."

But by the next night he was past that kind of fancy speech-making.

"Quit getting in a stew about nothing," he said. "Don't pay it no never mind."

Which was both strange grammar and an unfamiliar accent coming from him. Jane's husband was a lawyer now in Philadelphia. It had taken him a day and a night to pick up the accent and the idiom of a speech he couldn't have used at all since he was a child, *if* he had used it then. It had taken another full day for him to lose the half irony that made his new guise acceptable. It had taken another day and a very bad night (But she was so *nervous* visiting here for the first time. Didn't he even understand *that*?) for him to start in drinking. And now he wasn't shaving any more or brushing his teeth or changing his clothes or bothering to go down to the beach. And now he was always taking his mother's side.

They *did* look something alike. (Strangely. For wasn't it always the daughter who was supposed to end up looking more and more like the mother?) Sitting together side by side on the front porch, she with her empty hands folded, he with his clasping the almost empty glass, short, square-bodied, long-torsoed, they were clearly cut from the same pattern. Sometimes Harper's lips turned tight and down in precisely the same expression of unspoken disapproval. Sometimes, now, his small, quick, pale blue eyes reminded her of Mrs. Grim's. And Jane, slender ("Honey, you'll have to eat plenty while you're down here and put some meat on those bones. Harp, boy, you ought to be ashamed to let your wife get so frail and wispy."), milk-skinned and long-limbed, was beginning to feel made out of another substance, a member of another race.

At this moment, inspired by the sight of the flying pelicans, images to her at once of rigor and beauty and harmony and freedom, she felt like arguing.

"Now that you mention it, the Quigly children *are* beautiful."

Mrs. Grim grunted at that.

"Well, if you think naked savages are beautiful, you might say so. Each one to her own taste, as the old lady said."

"As a matter of fact, I *have* seen photographs of naked savages which I thought were beautiful, the savages that is," Jane persisted.

Harper stood up, sighed, and stretched.

"Tell you what," he said. "You want to see some savages around here? You just drop over to Black Bottom about ten o'clock on a Saturday night."

"That would cure her of notions," Mrs. Grim said, chuckling. She said the word *notions* as if it signified some kind of physical disease, barely mentionable in polite company. "That surely would cure her."

"You'd get yourself a bellyful of beautiful savages," Harper said.

"Where are you going?" Jane said.

"To pour myself another little drink. *If* you don't mind."

"Suit yourself," she said. "It's your vacation."

"Did you say *vocation*?"

"I did not."

"Much obliged."

Harper's mother rocked busily and steadily, looking straight ahead. Jane turned again to watch the fine line of the waves rising, hovering, exploding on the sand in snowy profusion. She heard Harper stumble over something in the kitchen and curse. Well, there was nothing to be done about it.

A whoop and a holler! A shrill pandemonium of treble cries and then a burst of sun-bronzed flesh as four blonde naked Quigly children shot around the corner of the porch, scattered like a flushed covey of quail down the path, and vanished in the dunes. Mrs. Grim was half out of her rocking chair, rigid, her face etched in lines of anger. Harper leaned on the door frame shaking his head.

"They won't never learn," he said.

"I tried to speak to the mother (*if* she is the mother) yesterday. And do you know she was *drunk*? Stone drunk in the middle of the day. I mean staggering around inside of that trailer blind drunk. No wonder those poor little children have to run around wild without a soul to look after them."

"They seem to be getting along all right, considering," Jane said.

"It's a wonder to me they don't all drown in the ocean," Mrs. Grim said. "I'd feel kind of sorry for The Man, if he wasn't so common and worthless himself. They tell me when he gets home from work the two of them start drinking together and just keep on until they pass out cold. The children just have to fend for themselves."

"Who told you that?"

"A perfectly legitimate source. Someone who ought to know," Mrs. Grim said indignantly.

"She didn't mean it to sound that way, Mother," Harper said. "She was just wondering."

Not even Jane now. Just *she.*

"I *did* mean it to sound that way," Jane said. "Gossip makes me sick."

"Well!" Mrs. Grim said.

"What in hell got into *you*?" Harper said.

117

"I don't know. I'm sorry. I just don't know."

Jane brushed past him running back toward the bedroom, fighting the impulse to tears. She flung herself on the bed and pulled a pillow over her head. It was a silly, childish gesture. He wasn't going to come running behind her and try to comfort her. He and his mother would talk about it in low voices, and after a while he'd come back to the bedroom and talk to her. He wouldn't offer any sympathy. And she was furious with herself that what she wanted was his sympathy.

She was confused about all of it she realized. It wasn't just the usual battle, the immemorial tug of war between mother-in-law and daughter-in-law. It was that all right, intensified by the inescapable fact that Harper was an only child. But it was other things as well. She was seeing her husband for the first time in his native environment, without the well-mannered, gentle, acquired protective coloration he wore in her world, a world of strangers to him. (What camouflage was there for her here?) He was different. He seemed to sense it too, to succumb in helpless fury to old pressures and forces. She felt that as long as they stayed here they were lost to each other. The man she had married and lived with was a ghost. The one in her bed at night now was not a very attractive stranger. In that sense Mrs. Grim had become in her eyes the evil enchantress of a child's fairy tale. But then, after all, the whole business was so childish!

Then there were the Quiglys, the Battleground. They lived, the whole tribe of them, in a small trailer behind the cottage and across a dirt road, just at the edge of a palmetto jungle. It was a sagging, worn-out trailer, set up on cinder blocks. And the yard, if you could call the littered and trampled space between the trailer and the road a yard, was a perfect mess. In the center of that space there was the cross-eyed wreck of an old Buick convertible. It never moved.

Sun baked it and the sudden summer showers soaked it. Every day Joe Quigly came home from work and washed and sponged it down, apparently to protect the paint and chrome from the salt air that corroded everything under the sun before long. After he'd finished, he'd climb in the driver's seat and just sit there. It looked (from the distance of the bedroom window where she always watched him) as if he pretended to be driving it. Maybe he had wrecked it and it wouldn't run any more. Maybe he had bought it as is from a junk yard and it didn't even have an engine. Maybe he simply didn't have the money for gas. (Which would be an odd thing for a bulldozer operator. She had heard they made lots of money. Unless . . . unless, maybe, alas, Mrs. Grim was quite right, and both Joe Quigly and his poor, frazzle-haired slattern of a wife, who usually appeared once a day anyway wrapped in an oversize pink dressing gown and wearing sneakers, blinking in the hard sunlight and stumbling over to the topless garbage can by the road to dispose of a bundle of—empty bottles?—*were alcoholics.*) In any case, Joe Quigly seemed to love that automobile and to be very possessive about it. If he found his children playing in it when he came trudging up the dirt road home, he ran and chased them out and away with kicks and blows and curses. They didn't seem to mind. They laughed and ran away and left him his car.

The strange thing to Jane was that neither did she. She should have cared. A man who mistreats his children! Of course he didn't really mistreat them. He had a tantrum and they had to flee, but it didn't seem to mean anything to them or, seriously, to him. It seemed to be a kind of game. It made her uneasy to think that she might have tolerated such a blow or kick or curse coming from him in just that spirit, though she was sure that if Harper ever struck her she would be badly hurt. Quigly was a curious one. Long, lean, shaggy-haired, his face high-boned, deeply tanned and lined, he moved around with a clumsy grace like an animal trying to walk on its hind legs. He grinned a snaggle- and yellow-tooth grin at her if they happened to pass, and he ran a hand through his thick, unruly blonde hair. He was a kind of caricature of the country bumpkin. But—and this was what touched and troubled her—there was something else, indefinable, about him that was utterly alien, yet intriguing. It was as if the clothes, the flesh and bones, the face he wore were all composite parts of a disguise, donned by choice and for some reason. Somehow he communicated a sense of elemental shiftlessness, of sly, supple and insinuative and irresponsible endurance. Thus the early gods, she thought, must have taken on their guise of mortal flesh and moved among us.

She had tried unsuccessfully to express this complex thing that she sensed to Harper after she'd seen Joe Quigly standing at the back door waiting for his quarter pound of butter and the electric iron. Harper had laughed at her.

"You artists! Him? He's a typical cracker boy. That's the way they all are. Godlike, my ass! Not worth a damn. Crooked as a bunch of snakes."

Since the bad night and the others following it when Harper tumbled into his side of the bed, dead drunk, and snored as soon as his face touched the pillow, she had discovered that she was increasingly fascinated by the myth she had made up for Joe Quigly. Oh, not in the ordinary way, to be sure. Not *that* way. But as one might be attracted by some wonderful new beast on display at the zoo. There was nothing to it, she assured herself, beyond that simple feeling of curiosity and delight.

Then yesterday something had happened. With Harper drinking and Mrs. Grim deep in a historical novel and Jane

120

restless and bored, she had gone for a long, lonely walk down the beach. She passed the last of the houses and the few bathers splashing in the surf, and she walked on, following the straight and narrow ribbon of soft sand that seemed to stretch, like some ultimate desert, to infinity. The sun felt warm and good. After a while, alone and happy, she sat down at the foot of a high dune to enjoy it, soon lay back and closed her eyes, dozing in the light. It seemed to penetrate her and fill her veins, and she imagined all her blood, streams, rivers, networks, and canals, as becoming a choir of pure molten gold. As she lay there in a complete blank pleasure, she heard at first dimly, then near and loud, a roaring sound, and she sat up just in time to avoid being buried alive by a falling mountain of sand. Choking and spluttering, she struggled to her feet with vague gestures like a drowning person and tried to brush away the sand which covered her. She looked around and then up above her. On top of the dune, poised perilously at the very edge of it, was the flat blade of the bull-dozer, and standing above and behind the blade, tall against the whirling sky, straddle-legged, with the afternoon sun glaring behind him, was Joe Quigly, his wild hair tousled by the sea breeze, his head tossed back laughing. Jane was furious. Though she was fully and modestly dressed in shorts and a T-shirt, she felt as if he'd been spying on her naked. And then to be covered up, nearly killed in fact, was no joke. Joe Quigly obviously felt differently about it, and, even if he guessed how she must feel, he didn't care. He was content to laugh at her, and she had to laugh too. She stood there looking up at him and laughing, and she shyly raised her hand to wave at him. He waved back, vanished, backed the bull-dozer away from the edge and went to work again.

Neither of them had said a word. Yet she was as pleased as if he'd tossed her a bouquet of flowers.

She kept that story to herself, not daring to mention it to Harper now. He was sure to take a different view of it.

Jane heard the bedroom door close behind her. She turned her head and saw Harper standing over her.

"I don't know what gets into you sometimes."

"I don't either," she said. "I'm sorry."

"You ought to be. That was pretty rude."

"I know it and I really am sorry."

He dropped down on his hands and knees on the floor and crawled under the bed. She heard him fumbling among the luggage they had stored there.

"What are you doing?"

"Looking for your box of paints," he said.

"What on earth for?"

"I got to paint me a sign."

"With those? That's too expensive."

"I'd be glad to use some other paint," he said. "But it happens we ain't got none. We've told these folks for the last time. Now I'm putting up a 'Keep Off' sign."

"That's silly, Harper. You've been drinking and that's a silly idea."

He backed out and raised his head to the level of the bed.

"You don't understand. Not at all," he said. "There happens to be a *legal* problem involved. If they keep on using the path and we don't put up a sign, then it becomes a common pathway. We don't want that, do we?"

"I guess not."

"Want to help me?" he said. "You can letter a whole lot better than I can."

"No," she said. "Just help yourself. The paints are right there somewhere."

"Where are you going?"

"Just for a walk," she said, shutting the door behind her.

She took the public approach to the beach and avoided the path to save herself from having to pass under the gray scrutiny of Mrs. Grim. She set off south at a good pace, feeling the warm sand between her toes. The tide was coming in now. Jane liked high tide best, though it was hard to explain why, even to herself. Somehow when the tide was high you felt you knew, were familiar with the things the water covered and concealed. At low tide shallow sloughs were mysteries. If you waded you were apt to step on something hidden there, some submarine creature, a quick, brittle, scuttling crab, a jellyfish. (She remembered with a shiver a story of someone stepping on a corpse in the surf.) High tide, though, seemed to be a blessing, the blue waves breaking over and finally covering the beach. The natural impulse of water. It seemed like a fine idea for water to want to cover the land. Perhaps that's how old Noah looked at it, she thought.

She almost tripped over a dead pelican and started back a step in surprise. It lay on the sand, a crumpled mass of wet feathers, a beak slack as a drunk's jaw, as an idiot's, bloody peepholes for eyes (the little birds had already plucked them like grapes), and crawling with black flies and small bugs. She was stabbed with a chill omen. She had to hold her nose as she stepped by.

After the last houses and the last bather—a great fat bald-headed man in a two-piece bathing suit bobbing and splashing like a happy hippo—she felt liberated at last. The sun glared on the empty sand ahead of her. She imagined herself as a pilgrim lost in a far land. It was almost blinding it was so bright, and the breeze had died down so that she could feel the heat of the sun. She started to run. She ran along the beach at the foot of the dunes, ran breathless until she heard the bulldozer working nearby above her.

123

She was panting and dripping with sweat, for it had been a long run. With nervous, clumsy fingers she took off her clothes. She looked back once to where the last houses were like small toys and saw not a soul now on the beach. She threw her clothes aside and didn't care, was suddenly drunk with the sea and the sun and the sky and her lonely freedom. She lay back and closed her eyes and let the sun bathe her. Her brain was blank and heat-struck, and her flesh crawled with rivulets of sweat. Would he come to the edge of the dune and stand tall and see her now? Would he laugh then, or be struck blind? Would he bury her alive under mountains of sand? It was a strange sweet dream.

She must have been dozing literally, for when she came to herself, the sun had gone behind the dunes and she was in shadow. The breeze had sprung up cool. She was goose-pimpled. The sand was uncomfortable and she felt cold and ashamed. She covered herself quickly with her hands and arms and looked around. Still no one on the beach. No one, thank God, had seen her there. No one, she was sure. What in the world had possessed her to do something like that? Crouching over, she slipped into her clothing and noticed, dismayed, that in her distraction, in her fierce haste, she had ripped off half the buttons of her shorts. She must have been insane.

When she was dressed again and had brushed the sand off her arms and legs, she was ready to start the long walk back. It was then that she heard the laughter, soft and mocking, heard as if at a great distance of time and space, like the light laughter of a ghost, like the memory of laughter. She looked up just in time to see four small blond faces, haloed by light, the Quigly children peering over the edge of the dune, disappear into the camouflage of even blonder, blown sea wheat. Stiff and ashamed, she walked briskly away, following now in reverse the path her bare feet had made in the sand.

When she had to pass the dead pelican again, lapped at, tumbled and turned by the incoming tide, she was afraid she was going to be sick.

It was nearly dark when she came up the back way to the cottage. He was in the red shell of a car, hands gripping the steering wheel, mouth wide open, driving in some furious daydream, and he didn't see her pass by. Her feet were hurting and she limped a little, but he had nothing, not even pity, to offer her. Just at the edge of the path, facing the trailer was a sign, crudely lettered with great smears of her good paint (a half-empty tube lay by the path), multi-colored, the squandered paint dripping away from the letters as if they had been written in blood:

KEEP OFF THIS HERE PATH!
This means you

And beneath this was drawn a skull and crossbones.

Jane opened the back door and went into the kitchen. She poured herself a drink of Harper's whiskey and tossed it off.

"Is that you?" he called.

"Yes" she said. "It's me. I mean it is I."

She walked through the house to the front porch. Harper was sitting in his mother's rocker with a double-barrel shotgun in his lap. He was vigorously cleaning it with an oily rag. Jane leaned against the door frame behind him in weariness and slack despair and watched him work. He jerked his head around and grinned at her.

"Did you see my sign? Did you see the sign I put up?"

"Yes," she said. "I saw it."

"I found Daddy's old shotgun in the closet," he went on. "Next time I'm going to shoot. They've been warned aplenty.

The next time one of them sets a foot on this land, I'm going to get me some tailfeathers."

Just then Mrs. Grim came bustling through the living room. She brushed past Jane as if she didn't see her, and her eyes, her small, pale blue eyes, were bright with triumph and pleasure. She put a box at the feet of her son.

"Honey boy," she cried. "I found the shells for the gun. I knew they were here somewhere and I found them."

a game of catch

On the way to the beach the two brothers began to argue. Naomi sat between them in the front seat of the convertible, Tee Jay's car, and ate candy bars. Naomi didn't drink or smoke, but when she was away from the girls' junior college where she was the basketball coach, when she was away from it all on a day like this, going to the beach without a worry in the world, she would stuff candy. Sometimes she ate so much she got sick. Tee Jay knew all about it. He was the one who brought a whole box of Baby Ruth's along for the trip. Courtney, the crazy one, brought her a flower. When they tooted the horn for her in the alley behind the gymnasium and she came running out of the back door smiling at them, it was Tee Jay who handed her a box of Baby Ruth's.

He knew about her sweet tooth. Courtney got out of the car to let her in and gave her the gardenia, one fifty-cent gardenia.

"What's this for?" Naomi said. "Are we going to a dance or something?"

"I don't know," Courtney said to Tee Jay. "Are we?"

Tee Jay ignored him. Half-smiling, he kept staring into Naomi's eyes, until she looked down at her flat shoes.

"Don't look at me," Tee Jay said. "It's *his* idea."

"I'll tell you what," Courtney said. "Why don't you eat it? For dessert, after you finish the candy, I mean."

Naomi laughed and clapped him on the back, hearty, comradely. What else could she do? That Courtney was something, you never knew what he might think of next. You never knew how to take anything he said. Besides, he was just out of the State Asylum. He had been in and out a couple of times. They said he was cured now, but you wouldn't know it. You couldn't be sure about a thing like that.

They drove along the highway to the east coast, and the brothers were arguing as usual. Naomi chewed candy and let the warm air trouble her hair. It was dark and cut close, but with the breeze fingering it, combing it, she imagined it was long and blowing in a dark cloud like smoke behind her, long and mysterious as Lady Godiva's. Floating on her skirt between the firm bulge of her thighs, the gardenia was already turning brown at the edges, but it was sweet.

"I don't care where you read it," Tee Jay was saying. "It sounds like crap to me."

"I'm telling you that something like that, a murder, is just love in disguise. He might have just kissed them. It would be the same thing."

"Books! Books! That's all I get from you. Do you believe everything you read in a book?"

128

"He's got a thing about books, you know," Courtney said to Naomi. "Do you know the only book Tee Jay ever read? I mean *read*, all the way, every word from the beginning to the end."

"Don't try and involve me in the discussion," Naomi said, her mouth rich with chocolate.

She had been listening vaguely to their words, but it was all so morbid. They were arguing about some old man who had gathered his whole family together for a photograph, sat them down in a tight group on his front steps, his wife, his grown children, even his grandchildren. When he had them all ready and posed for the picture, he excused himself for just one moment and went back in the house. He returned with a shotgun, and before any of them could even move, he fired both barrels into them point blank. He was reloading the gun to shoot himself when the next-door neighbor came running over and knocked him out with a shovel. The papers were full of it. They were always full of things like that. And Naomi couldn't care less. Trust old Courtney to bring up the subject. Trust him, too, to try and get her in the argument.

"I'll tell you the only book Tee Jay ever read all the way through. It was called *The Bitter Tea of General Yen*."

"So what," Tee Jay said. "It wasn't a bad book."

"How would *you* know? What have you got to compare it with?"

"Look," Tee Jay said. "You're the one with the college education. I'm the one that went to work. I don't have time to read a lot of books. All I do is pay for the books you read."

"It doesn't take a lot of time to read a book," Courtney said.

"It takes too much time for me."

Naomi licked the candy off her fingers and reached forward and turned on the radio. When it warmed up, she twisted the dial until she found some music playing, then she turned it up as loud as it would go. It roared over and around them like a storm, scattering music to the four winds. She saw their mouths still moving furiously, but *they* couldn't hear each other if *she* couldn't, sitting between them. Courtney leaned close and whispered in her ear.

"Flaming Youth," he said.

"What?" she mouthed.

"Flaming Youth," he whispered again. "It's a sort of a joke."

Then he stuck out his wet tongue and fluttered it in her ear, and she jerked away from him. If it had been anyone else in the world but poor Courtney, she would have slapped his fresh face. Tee Jay, who was turning down the radio, missed the whole thing.

"Reach in the glove compartment," he said. "Hand me my cigarettes."

"I'd prefer if you didn't smoke," Naomi said. "You know how I feel about it."

"Who cares how you feel?" Tee Jay snapped at her, taking the pack from Courtney. "Maybe *I* don't like candy. Maybe it makes me sick to watch people who eat candy. I don't have the right to object, do I?"

"Candy is altogether different," Naomi said. "If God had intended for you to smoke, He would have made you a chimney."

"Yeah? Yeah?" Tee Jay said, lighting his cigarette. "Maybe you'd like to walk to the beach. If God had intended for you to ride, He would have put wheels on your ass."

Naomi glared straight ahead.

"It makes me sad to be the only one who isn't indulging in something, some lonely, stupid, solitary, ineffable private vice."

And with that curious remark Courtney simply put his

130

hand in her lap and took the gardenia. He held it under his nose, sniffed it, and then began to chew the white bitter petals.

"Don't *swallow* it!" Naomi cried. "What's the matter, are you crazy?"

She blushed then, realizing that it had just slipped out like that.

"Oh no," Courtney said, his mouth white and full of flower. "I *used* to be, but I'm not any more. I'm just as sane as everyone."

Inexplicably, Tee Jay laughed.

"How does it taste, boy?" he said.

"Not too bad," Courtney said. "On the other hand, don't feel that you're missing out on anything."

"You better be careful," Naomi said. "I've heard tell they're poison."

"You'll never know for sure until somebody tries one," Courtney said. "That's science for you."

After that they rode without talking, just listening to the music on the radio. Naomi felt a lot better now that they had stopped arguing. The only trouble was still Courtney. He kept putting his hand on her leg. That would be all right, just resting there, but he wouldn't leave well enough alone. After a while, all of a sudden, he'd stiffen all his fingers at once and start edging up her thigh like a spider, sort of on tiptoes or tipfingers. When his hand got too close for comfort, sneaking toward the ultimate destination which Naomi, in spite of all, to her dying day, would call her privates, plural, she would have to take his hand firmly in hers and remove it. Then the whole process would begin all over again. Courtney kept looking straight up the road, and so did she. She didn't want to make a scene, and she knew if Tee Jay noticed anything, he'd stop the car and beat Courtney up.

When they got to the beach it seemed like a perfect day. The sun was bright, the water was blue and scaled with the whitecaps of a brisk east wind. The tide was down, but rising, so they could still drive up and down the beach in Tee Jay's good-looking car. Far out along the horizon clouds like dark bruises were massing and swelling, but they were a long way away. They drove up and down the beach a few times, slowly, just looking at the people, the children running and jumping and splashing and throwing sand, as shrill and swift as gulls, the muscular young men, bronzed and cocky, the girls in their bright bathing suits, and, too, the old people, the fat and the thin, misshapen and grotesque, sprawled under beach umbrellas, or burning lurid shades of pink in the sun. The men with mountainous stomachs and the little jiggly breasts like girls at puberty, and bandy, veined legs, and the women, thin and wrinkled as old, cracked leather, or enormous, all rippling, shaking bellies and buttocks, and great breasts sagging like overripe fruit, disgusted Naomi. She could not stand to look at them. *They* had a nerve, exposing themselves like that! Still, she was irresistibly fascinated; she couldn't help studying them and wondering, with an inner chill as if her blood had turned to quicksilver, if she would ever be like that.

After they had driven up and down a while, Tee Jay turned south and drove past the last of the cottages, clinging to the dunes precariously like driftwood on the swelling sea, past the last of the swimmers, the last lifeguard, dozing and golden on his stilted perch, to the open beach.

"Where are we going now?" Naomi asked.

"Swimming," Tee Jay said.

"Well," she said, "I'd like to go to the bathhouse and put on my bathing suit."

"The bathhouse? Christ, what *for*?"

"Turn the car around, please," she said.

"That's the craziest thing I ever heard of," Tee Jay said. "The bathhouse costs fifty cents apiece. We can dress in the dunes for free."

"I'd *prefer* to dress in the bathhouse."

"What's the *matter* with you? Courtney won't mind."

"Can't you see the girl is moved by natural modesty?" Courtney said. "Take her to the bathhouse."

"Natural modesty, my ass! Fifty cents is a whole lot of money to fork over all of a sudden just because for the first time in her life Naomi decides she's modest."

"Women are that way," Courtney said. "Full of little surprises."

He only said that, Naomi knew, because of the way his own wife had done him. After three years of married life and two children, she simply left one day, drove off with Billy Towne who was a salesman of fishing tackle up and down both coasts, from Fernandina to Coral Gables, from Pensacola to Key West. Yes, Billy Towne could take Maxine all over the whole state. She could go to the beaches while he was working, and at night they could go to all the bars and nightclubs. It was a good life for her. The thing was how hard it hit Courtney. He worshipped Maxine, like a fool, because anybody could have told him how she was born a bitch and would die a bitch, no matter how pretty she was. So away went Maxine, *with* the two little girls, living in open unashamed sin with that Billy Towne. And *poof!* Courtney was in the State Asylum. Then *she* could divorce him because he was legally crazy. Oh yes, he would make all of those nasty cracks about women in general, but the world knew that if Maxine crooked her little finger at him, he'd go back to her on his hands and knees. Tee Jay, of course, had never married anybody. He hadn't even mentioned marriage in all this time. Still, there was always the chance that he would.

"I'm sorry," Naomi said, "but I really would rather dress at the bathhouse. I'll pay for it myself."

"In *that* case—" Tee Jay said.

And he turned the car around in a wild, wide, sand-scattering circle and sped back toward the main beach. He hunched over the wheel, close to the windshield like a racing driver, and put the gas pedal to the floor. That was Tee Jay for you!

Once inside the small unpainted cubicle in the bathhouse, standing on the wet, strutted slats, Naomi undressed and hung her clothes on a nail. She was a tall ungainly girl. Her face, though cast in large, coarse features, had a uniformity that made her seem conventionally pretty. But her body was oddly proportioned. Her thick, heavy-muscled legs, her hard high large buttocks, and her flat stomach seemed to belong to someone much larger, perhaps even, except for the curve of her hips, to a powerful man. ("My fullback," Tee Jay called her.) Her upper body was slight and frail-boned, flat-chested like a young girl's. In her clothes, wearing full skirts, loose peasant blouses, and flat shoes, she achieved a kind of equilibrium, but at moments like this, alone and naked, she felt a shame and self-revulsion that nearly brought her to tears. She struggled into her black, one-piece suit, too tight at the hips, padded at the breasts, put on her white bathing cap, and placed the elastic-banded key around her wrist. She pulled the door of the cubicle to, sharply, behind her.

The two of them were waiting for her in the car. They turned their heads together and stared at her as she came across the boardwalk and down the wooden steps and across the powdery sand near the dunes. She began running toward them.

134

"Look," Courtney cried, "a female centaur. Whatever that may be."

"Let's get the show on the road," Tee Jay said.

Then, still staring at her as she got into the car, Courtney said, "Cough drops."

When Tee Jay found a place that suited him, out of sight of the main beach, the two of them took their swimming trunks and went up into the dunes to change. Naomi spread out a beach blanket and covered her exposed skin with suntan oil. She had a little plaid beach basket from which she took a pair of dark glasses and a confession magazine. Just then, settling comfortably in the sunlight, she heard the thunder and felt the breeze coming stronger and cooler off the ocean, saw lightning far off in the clouds and whitecaps flickering across the whole expanse of the visible sea.

"It's going to squall," she called.

"So what?" Tee Jay replied from the dunes.

And she looked and saw the two of them, the twins, standing side by side on top of a dune, perfectly identical except that Courtney was pale and soft beside Tee Jay. They came charging down in a little whirlwind of sand and legs, leapt right over her and past with flashing heels and flanks, raced into the water. Soon they were splashing each other and shouting, but she couldn't hear what they were saying to each other. She went back to the car and got the box of Baby Ruth's. She returned and, opening her magazine, began to read the sad thrilling tale of an innocent girl who was seduced by a state policeman.

By the time the two came back from their swim, they were arguing again, and about the same old thing. Tee Jay opened the glove compartment and produced a pint of whiskey. They both had a drink. A lot they cared about her approval! Then Tee Jay went around and opened the trunk. He fumbled around until he found a softball and two gloves. It

135

was a brand new softball, white, hard, and shiny.

"You want to play catch?"

"No," she said. "I don't feel much like it right now."

"*Well*, how do you like that?"

"I'll throw a few with you," Courtney said.

They moved out in front of the car and began to lob the ball easily, back and forth. Tee Jay was the athlete. He played third base for Morrison's Department Store Softball Team. Naomi loved to go and watch him play on a spring or summer evening under the lights, in his red and green and gold uniform. He was so quick, so deft, so dandy around the bag. He was the only man she had ever seen, except in newsreels and such, that she could really *admire* when he was playing a game. The others, even the good ones, were so sloppy and careless, like they didn't care, like it was so easy for them, running and throwing and just being men, like they didn't give two hoots what anybody thought. She hated them. Tee Jay was nervous and quick and delicate; every move he made seemed to have its reason. Naomi's heart leapt for him when she saw him move swiftly to snag a hard-hit ball, or when he came running full speed, but like a dancer on points, to scoop up a bunt, whirl, and in the same motion burn it down to second or to first base. Courtney, on the other hand, had never been much at sports. That was a funny thing. The first time he was at the State Asylum he got the notion somehow that he was going to play shortstop for the New York Yankees. It was terrible. Tee Jay would have to drive up there and spend whole weekends batting him flies and grounders and playing catch with him. At least, Naomi noticed, he had improved from the practice. She returned to her magazine story.

The storm moved in on them. Drops of rain began to fall, and, looking up, Naomi saw that the black clouds were overhead and all around them. They seemed to be shaggy and running like buffaloes in the movies. The waves were much bigger now and broke on the sand with huge crashes and bursts of foam like breaking glass. She bundled her things together and ran to the car. She pulled the lever that controlled the mechanism, and the gray top began to creak forward into place.

"Who told you to do that?" Tee Jay yelled at her.

He ran over, his face pinched and flushed with anger, and let the top down again. The rain was falling harder now, in thick drops. The trouble was that they had started the argument again.

"Cut off your nose to spite your face," she said. But a lance of lightning and a barrage of thunder drowned out her voice.

"What was that? What did you say?"

"Never mind," she replied.

She crouched in the front seat and the cold rain fell on her. The two of them, heedless of rain, thunder, and lightning, stood there shouting at each other and throwing the ball as hard as they could. They had thrown their gloves aside. They shouted and threw the ball so hard she didn't see how they could catch it barehanded. It was very very dangerous for all of them, she knew. She'd heard stories about people being struck by lightning on the beach. Besides the tide was rising; pretty soon they wouldn't be able to drive back along the beach. She got out of the car and ran to Tee Jay.

"Let's go," she said. "Let's go home."

Tee Jay threw the ball to Courtney. He threw it gently.

"Let's quit," Tee Jay said. "This is crazy."

"Are you *afraid?*" Courtney yelled.

The full strength of the squall was on them now. With the rain pelting, the high wind and the lightning and thunder, they had to scream to each other. Courtney fired the ball back to Tee Jay and he threw it back just as hard. Naomi could see the red round shape of the ball printed on Tee Jay's palm and fingers.

"*You* catch it," Courtney screamed at her. "You're the coach."

She caught it and threw it to Tee Jay. Then it was a three-cornered game. For a few minutes she was glad to be shielding Tee Jay, catching that wet, hot, skin-wincing ball and throwing it, easy, to him. But it hurt and Tee Jay seemed impatient to throw again. He didn't seem to appreciate what she was doing at all. So she threw it to him as hard as she could.

"Damn you!" he said.

Her hands were bruised and aching, and she was afraid of the thunder and lightning, but still they kept throwing the ball so fast that she didn't know what to do. Finally Courtney dropped one and it rolled away down the beach. He chased after it, and she was running behind him. When he seized it and spun around, wild-eyed, to throw it to her, she was close enough to kiss him if she had wanted to. Surprised, he started back. The tears started streaming from her eyes.

"Please, please, let's stop now and go home."

"No," he said. "No, we aren't going to stop."

"Please," she said. "Please."

He squeezed the ball in both hands.

"All right," he said. "I'll tell you what. You take off your bathing suit, and we'll go home."

"Throw the God-damn ball!" Tee Jay yelled.

Courtney waved at him to wait a minute. Tee Jay stamped his feet angrily, but waited.

"Go on, take it off," Courtney said to her.

"Will we go home then?"

He nodded.

138

She undid her shoulder straps and slipped and wriggled out of the rain-soaked suit. It lay like a small shadow at her feet.

"Now dance."

"What?"

"When I brought you the flower, you made a joke about going to a dance. Well, this is it. Dance for me."

Clumsily, cold, shivering in the wind, and still crying, she began to dance. Courtney laughed at her. He reached out and touched her small, brown, shrunk nipples with his fingers.

"See what I mean about cough drops?" he said. Then he cupped his hands and yelled into the wind to Tee Jay. "See what I mean? See what I mean about love? I *love* her."

"Never mind all that crap," Tee Jay replied. "Just keep throwing the God-damn ball and we'll see who's afraid around here."

Naomi knelt down then, beside her bathing suit, and hid her face. She huddled on her self like a child asleep, and the two men continued to throw the ball back and forth with unrelenting fury.

hawk in the april wind

Because it was early spring the whole land dreamed it was awake. The air on this morning was sweet and new. It had rained hard the night before, a real gulley-washer sluicing the clay around the high hillside farm where she lived, a scary, wild, windy rain with the lightning suddenly turning the whole room white as a ghost, and when she looked out of the window she saw the tall pines tossing their green manes like frightened horses.

Bird song, clear and cold and precise, was what she woke to, and soft sunlight and a rinsed air haunted with the most sweet and subtle odors. She stretched in her bed and felt herself from tips of toes to roots of hair all atingle, glowing and growing, but small and new too, a taut, hard being like a bud about to explode into some pure color or languor, like a clenched fist about to fall apart and become an easy, open palm.

It was the air, she knew, the air like wild honey or wild grapes that turned her head so to thoughts of herself and what she was becoming.

When she went barefoot across the muddy space of ground, feeling the good sticky clay crawling between her toes, with the empty bucket to fill it at the pump, she drank the air and flung back her head, tossed her loose, long hair and looked up into the dazzling heart of the sky, blue as the core of a match flame. It was a dizzy sight, a spinning feeling, to look up so high and see the lean white clouds, no more than veils or wisps of stuff really, chasing each other over the world. She thought then that if she hadn't had the soft wet clay on her feet, if she hadn't been so rooted like a young tree in the earth, she might have pushed off easy and dived straight into the sky and disappeared. It would have been an easy thing to do, light and easy like falling in a dream.

Coming back from the pump, she was so lighthearted, so weak in the knees and frail, that she staggered with the simple weight of the bucket. It might as well have been a stone or a heavy log.

Now she was carrying a tin pail of buttermilk and coming down from the farm to the highway. She crossed the pasture —the old cow eyed her with a soft, wet glance and went on chewing—slipped through the fence and took the twisty path down through the woods. The woods were still dark, dripping from the rain, chilly as a cave, and full of rich strange smells. Like the cave where some animal has slept. She walked modestly, head down, watching the path in front of her feet, looking neither left nor right, shrinking into herself as if she could become so small that she couldn't be seen. Because then, if she went through on tiptoes, one of the trees wouldn't reach out with a long green arm and snatch her away forever.

That was the game she had played with the trees when she was a child. Now she was not a child, but she knew without thinking about it that she owed them that much still until she was finally all grown, really *grown up*.

When the path came out of the woods, under the sky with a view of the mountains and a peek at the highway far below, just a single white curve of the road to be seen like a bare shoulder, she relaxed again, stretched tall, and began to run down the steep path, not caring about anything, not caring whether or not she tripped on a root or a rock and fell all the way down in bits and pieces like old humpty-dumpty, not caring either, for that wonderful moment, whether or not she spilled the can of buttermilk and tumbled head over heels into a bramble patch, and so, not caring, running no risk at all.

She stopped short and almost fell. Flung her arm around a little pine tree and danced all around it to keep from pitching headlong, and pulled up short and trembling. Because she saw somebody right smack in the middle of the highway where she would have to cross over, a man alone in the middle of the road cupping his hand over his eye to look up and see *her*. She crouched behind the tree and studied him. He was a young man, it looked, from the free and easy way he carried himself, and a stranger from the kind of clothes he was wearing. He had lost her now that she was behind the tree, must be wondering where in the world she had vanished to. She giggled.

Well, she could stay here safe and sound until he gave up looking and started along the road. Or she could always go back higher. Or she could simply keep going down the path

142

and cross the highway right under his nose, ignoring him. That seemed like the thing to do. It made her smile to picture it. She would come down the path ever so slowly, dainty-footed as a heifer, and he would be waiting. But when she got there and he smiled at her and wanted to talk, she would pass right by him as if she didn't even have the time of day or a nod for him. And *he*, he would think that maybe she didn't see him at all or maybe that there was nothing to see, that he was invisible and wasn't any more to be seen than a breath of air.

That would surely serve him right for standing in the middle of the road and watching her fling herself down the path in pure abandon when she didn't know that anyone else was looking.

Down she went, tight-lipped and determined to pass him by, but when he said his hello to her in an accent she had never heard, she found that she stopped at the edge of the road and smiled back at him.

"When you came running out of the trees up there," he said, "I thought for sure you were going to fall and break your neck. Was something chasing you?"

She shook her head, still smiling.

He was a funny-looking boy, about her own age, she guessed, though he was dressed like a man, in the gray-and-white striped city suit, like a lawyer or a preacher or a salesman or a government man, and it *was* somebody else's suit because he was a skinny little thing and the coat hung halfway to the ground and he had rolled up the cuffs of his sleeves so his hands could be seen. He had on little black-and-white, pointed city shoes too, not the kind a man could work in or even take much of a walk in. He had a pinched pale face, like a bird's, and a lot of tumbling loose dark hair like a wet mop. He *did* look strange and she thought maybe he was a gypsy or something. She would have been shy and

143

afraid except that he had such a bright smile and such pale, light-filled eyes.

"There's bears up in the woods," she said, astonished at the sound of her own voice coming out loud and clear as if she made a habit of meeting strangers and talking with them.

He looked up into the woods and seemed to shiver. She noticed he was soaking wet, so he must have been walking all night or maybe sleeping out in the rainstorm, in the woods somewhere.

"They aren't liable to bother you," she said to reassure him. "They're shy too."

"That's good," he said laughing.

She thought it was all finished and stooped to pick up the pail of buttermilk she had set down, but he still had something to say to her.

"Don't a car or a truck ever come along this road?"

"Surely," she said. "Every once in a while."

"That's good too," he said. "I thought maybe I'd have to walk all the way to Hendersonville."

"That's a good long walk," she said. "You'd be a while getting there."

He looked down at his thin, fancy shoes and sighed. His feet must be hurting him. He came over to the side of the road and sat down near her. He unlaced his shoes and rubbed his feet. She wondered what to do, then sat down too.

"What do you have in that pail?"

"Buttermilk," she said. "For my grandma."

He looked at the pail, beaded and cool. He reached into a pocket of his coat and pulled out a sandwich wrapped in wax paper.

"I'll tell you what," he said. "I'll trade you a piece of this sandwich for a drink of that milk."

"I ain't hungry," she said.

Then as she looked at her bare feet and wiggled her dirty

144

toes, it occurred to her that maybe the reason he said that was that *he* was thirsty.

"I couldn't do that," she said. "Grandma would get mad and my daddy would be just liable to take a switch to me."

"Isn't there some place where a man could get a drink of water?"

"There's a store up the road about two miles where they got running water and soda pop and everything."

"Where do you live?"

She tossed her head in the direction she had come from.

"'Bout a mile yonder, up through the woods."

"Maybe I could get a drink there."

"Not likely," she said. "If my daddy didn't get you, my brothers would for sure."

He burst out laughing, hard and harsh.

"This is some country you live in. If the bears don't get you, the bad men will."

"It ain't so bad if you live here."

"I would just like to see some of that famous southern hospitality," he said. "The only thing anybody give me for free since I got here is this sandwich. A truck driver gave me that. He was from New Jersey."

"That's a long way away," she said.

He looked so woebegone, wet and shabby, hungry and tired, and he kept sneaking looks at the pail of milk that she knew before she got safely across the highway she would weaken and give him a drink even if it did mean a switching across her bottom with a whistling green branch. It made her tingle there, as if she had been switched already, and made her feel a little ashamed because she thought it would be worth it after all. But, whether or no, she wasn't going to give up easy.

"What you got besides that sandwich to trade?"

He was lacing up his shoes again. He was having trouble

145

too. Poor fool, didn't he know how fast feet would swell if you took them out of a pair of tight shoes?

"I don't have anything," he said. "Not money if that's what you mean."

"You're making a long trip without any money?"

"Oh, I'll get money all right. I'll work and get plenty of money. Next time I come down *this* road—if I ever have to come down this godforsaken road again—I'll be driving a big car of my own. You won't see me for the dust."

"You're pretty young to have a car of your own," she said, sadly picturing herself standing by the road in the dust to let him go past with his nose in the air, at the wheel of something so long and gleaming and shining it couldn't be believed.

"Huh!" he snorted. "I'm sixteen. How old are you?"

"Fourteen."

"You're just a child," he said in most superior way.

"Be fifteen in May."

He took a cigarette out of a crumpled pack, lit it, and lay back against the bank by the road, smoked and looked up into the sky.

"I see you got a pretty watch," she said. It was a glinty, silvery thing on his wrist.

"You want my watch for a drink of buttermilk? That beats everything."

"Depends on how thirsty you are."

He rolled over on his side and propped his weight on his elbow to look at her. He was smiling again as if she had said the funniest thing in the world. She decided to give up on the watch. She didn't really mean it anyhow, but it was something to try.

"What *do* you have?"

"Nothing," he said. "Just nothing at all. Unless you smoke cigarettes."

146

"Don't touch them," she said. Then standing up, shaking the stiffness out of her young, thin legs: "Well, I guess that's that."

"I'll give you a kiss for a drink of that buttermilk."

She stiffened and looked down into his grinning face.

"I wouldn't do that," she said. "Nobody has ever kissed me."

In an instant he was standing up beside her, not really as tall as she was, but that was all right because he had a nice swaggery way about him like a little banty rooster that was bound to please, and his dark hair close had a sweet funny smell to it like perfume. She let him kiss her on the lips and wasn't ashamed, though she was glad, too, that nobody she knew was there to see it happen.

"All right," she said. "You can have a drink, but don't take much."

He took the pail and drank, leaving a fine white mustache above his lips.

"Was that really the first time?"

"Yes," she said defensively. "We live in a kind of a lonesome place."

"It was all right, wasn't it? A fair trade?"

"If you don't drink too much of the milk."

"Would you trade again?"

This time she had to think about it, but she decided that as long as he was probably going to drink half of it anyway she might as well.

So they traded some kisses and he drank most of the milk and ate his sandwich. He looked a little better. She was thinking that if he had enough to eat and some clothes to wear that fit him better, he would be a good-looking boy, even if he was short. It was probably the smoking that stunted his growth, and a thing like that couldn't be helped. She would like to have stood there and talked with him awhile more, but now that he had what he wanted in the first place she knew that he was all itching to be off to Hendersonville. She dallied to delay him.

"What's it like in Hendersonville?"

"Don't know," he said. "Haven't you ever been there?"

"Nope," she said. "I imagine you've been a lot of places, though."

"I sure have. I've been a lot of places and I'm going to be in a lot more before I'm done."

"Don't you have any notion of just stopping somewhere, some place you could like, and *staying* there?"

"Not me," he said. "I'll never stop any place for long."

"Pity," she said.

He was ready to go now, she was sure. He was trembling to be on his way again and leave her behind. It made her sad, but it made her feel good, too, that he didn't just turn his back on her and go off, that he wanted to leave her nicely, with some kind of manners.

"What's your name?"

"Elizabeth," she said.

"That's a nice name."

"What's yours?"

With that he kissed her again, not a real kiss, just a peck on the cheek and a pat of his hand on her back, and a bright, scornful smile.

"Pudding Tame," he said, and walked away quickly, just as he should have, lively and funny in his suit and funny with all his farfetched ideas and crazy dreams. At the curve where the road bent out of sight he turned once and waved at her before he disappeared.

She stood looking at the spot where he had been with the almost-empty milk pail dangling in her hands. Then she smiled to herself and ran across the road and started up the steep path on the other side.

148

High up, above the treetops, was a brown chicken hawk, small, mean, and lazy, riding the breeze. He'd be looking for a plump hen to put his claws into or, more likely, some chickies. His shadow was pure trouble and it was the right thing, she knew, that her father would run out of the house with his shotgun when a hawk came around.

But just today, a strange and silly day when the whole land dreamed it was awake and the air was like wild honey and grapes, she gave her heart to the hawk and couldn't have cared less whether it hurt or not.

goodbye, goodbye,
be always kind
and true

At first Peter Joshman hadn't known what to make of it all, how to take it. In the beginning came the scouts, surveyors and engineers, crisp in khaki, their white pith helmets shining, driving State-owned trucks and jeeps, and supported by little galaxies of rodmen and assistants in T-shirts. They came to look at the lay of the land, studied it, measured it, marked it and departed. Then (and it was not long afterwards) came the axes, the bulldozers, and the dynamite. They shook the earth and rattled the window panes, jarred cups and glasses on the shelves, troubled old things from accustomed places with their labors, and left behind them a clay-colored raw swathe cut through the intense monotonous green of the pine

150

woods and across the fields from West to East, like a new scar, so close he could have thrown a stone from his chair on the porch and landed it in the center with a little puff or plume of dust. After that the big machines, the rollers and levellers and graders, hurried through the early spring, smoothing the wound that had been made in his field of vision. There were men in khaki and explorers' helmets again, overseeing, writing and writing on their clipboards, and there were the young men, all lithe arrogance and bronzed bravado as, shirtless in the Florida sun, wheeling their huge machines, laughing brilliantly and shouting profanely at each other, they created a dusty chaos.

Inevitably the convicts from the State Camp followed, sweating men, black and white, in gray prison uniforms, with their shovels and rakes and pick mattocks, working slowly forward day by day along the smoothed earth, spreading gravel and finally the asphalt (that smelled at first good enough to eat), all under the scrutiny of the squat, relaxed, almost motionless guards who peered squint-eyed from beneath broad-brimmed hats into the glare of light studying the work, cradling their shotguns lightly in their arms like living things. One of the convicts, a trusty probably, had come to the house for a bucket of water and Peter Joshman jabbed with his cane in the direction of the pump.

"What's a man like you doing with a walking cane?" the convict asked him. "You ain't *that* old, is you?"

"I'm a wounded man."

"Somebody shot you?"

"Sure they did," Peter said. "In the war, the first one. I got a wooden leg, but you wouldn't know it."

"No, you wouldn't to look at you," the convict said. "Now you got it made, though, huh? Sit on your ass and draw a government pension."

"This here's my son-in-law's house," Peter said. "This here

is *his* farm. I can't do no heavy work. I can't do much of nothing but sit in my rocker and watch things."

"Well, you going to have something to look at from now on with this new highway."

"I don't know as I can get used to what they done. It takes me a while to get used to things."

"Hell!" the convict said, moving now towards the pump. "After a while you can get used to most anything."

"You don't have to *like* it though," Peter Joshman said, laughing, surprised to hear himself laughing out loud like that. "No sir, you don't have to like it a damn' sight."

They poured the sweet thick asphalt and they rolled it and levelled it, and it was really a road. Pretty soon the tourists would be coming down it, making a short-cut to the East Coast with its splendid beaches, the sun and waves and sand as white and fine as sugar there. Peter sat in his rocker, gripping his heavy cane with knuckles whitened from impotent anger, and saw them finish the job. Some people seemed to like it fine. The children, his grandchildren, and all the devious wolf-pack of them from the other farms around, ran when they could with shrill excitement—like a flock of little birds, they were so swift and aimless—around the fringes of all the action. They would be happy to see the cars come by. And up at Evergreen, the nearest crossroads town, the gas station owner, the storekeeper, and even the preacher took it for a good sign that now they were going to have a real paved highway passing through. His son-in-law, S. Jay, took it badly. They had gouged a piece of his land, split one field in two, and though it meant some cash money for him, it meant fencing too, and crossing the highway to do his work.

"What good does it do me, anyhow?" S. Jay grumbled. "I never go to the beach anyway, except on the Fourth of July."

"Get a new car, Daddy," the children hollered and pestered. "Get us a new car."

152

"Sure," he replied. "And while I'm at it I might just as well buy me a patch of ground on the moon."

"We could set up a stand by the road," his wife (old Peter's daughter) said. "We could make money selling garden vegetables and fresh eggs."

"This is nothing but a long lonely stretch of straight road," S. Jay answered. "Those folks won't even slow down under sixty. They got something else in mind. Fresh vegetables! Eggs!"

"Well, it's an idea."

"Won't anything come of it. Who's going to build you a shack to sell from?"

"And maybe the children could sell ice-cold lemonade."

"Lemonade!" S. Jay snorted. "Oh my God! You don't know nothing about this world, nothing at all."

Still, Peter thought that they ought to do *something*. It's hard, it's wrong even, he thought, to sit still and watch a great change, something new and something that will never, in one lifetime, be the same again, and not give at least a signal or a sign of approval or discontent. When the cars at last began to come, shiny new ones, convertibles with their tops down so that he could see the bright relaxed people in their bright unlikely clothes heading to and from the ocean, hear the radios playing, hear the rhythms of their voices and occasionally the burst of their laughter, then he suddenly felt better about the whole thing. That was entirely different, a road with *people*. Suddenly everything was happening. He'd hear them coming, and they'd flash into his view, and tires humming or purring or swishing with a sound like tearing cloth, and the sun exploding in little balls of brightness off the gloss and chrome of auto bodies, and, for a fabulous instant, he saw them in profile, lean as arrows in flight, going or coming, framed against the green pines, the rich green fields they crossed.

153

It came to him that he ought to *participate*, share in some way that hurtling unbelievable moment of gleaming speed. He wanted to offer his benediction. So, he had the boys, his grandchildren, move the rocker out in the front yard, close to the road, under the shade of a mulberry tree where he could wave at them and they, seeing him, could wave back. They smiled and laughed, shouted or waved in solemn silence, and the children, the children always seemed to catch his signal and return it.

S. Jay was a little angry, a little ashamed.

"It must be nice," he said, "it must be *mighty* nice to have nothing to do with yourself but sit by the side of the road and watch the cars go by."

And Peter Joshman, in spite of himself, sensitive of his position as a paying guest in the house, lonely too, fell upon self-pity grimly:

"Lose *your* leg sometime and see how you like it."

"S. Jay don't mean any harm, Daddy," his daughter said. "You know how *he* is."

"Never mind about that leg," S. Jay said. "I don't grudge you a thing. But it seems like you could find something besides just sitting and waving at strangers. What do those folks mean to you anyhow?"

"They cease to be strangers when I see them pass by."

"Listen," S. Jay said. "Those folks are laughing at you. You're a joke."

"It don't do nobody no harm," Peter said. "It does me a whole world of good."

"It isn't even *good* for you, Daddy," his daughter said, siding at last with her husband. "You ought to sit in the shade of the porch, at least."

"They won't be able to see me from the road."

"Well, why don't you hang up a sign or something?" S. Jay said. "Run up a flag."

"Don't laugh at him, Jay," his daughter said. "It's wrong to make fun of an older man like that."

"He makes fun of hisself."

Still, it was S. Jay who put the notion in his mind. Why *not* sit comfortable in the shade of the porch and still have a way to communicate with them, the drivers and the riders? How to do this, with wit and wisdom, was his problem. Wisdom, yes; for what stranger, moving however swiftly over whatever strange or alien landscape, where he knows no one, owns nothing, between departure and arrival, is not touched, deeply, by a salute, a sign of some kind from a stranger by the road saying *I acknowledge you as flesh and blood, as a creature of dust and breath like myself. You're not a thing that happens to my eyes. You're not like the road.* Saying to himself like the children, his grandchildren, saying to himself, to be truthful, like the song they always sing at the end of Sunday school—"Goodbye, Goodbye, be always kind and true." But to say this with wit because (and Peter Joshman knew this, though often irascible, embittered too, and, like everyone, self-pitying) he knew that a shared truth needs a disguise. Laughter will do. Otherwise, like Adam and Eve without the wit of fig leaves, the naked truth would shame to the quick.

The beginning was more or less accidental. An old dressmaker's dummy was in the barn from the days when first his wife and then his daughter, now another man's wife and the mother of her own children, sewed for a living. It was an easy thing to dress the dummy in his old-fashioned Army uniform, to place it on a stump at the edge of the road, to rig the right arm something like his own artificial leg so that, sitting on his rocker on the porch, he could at just the right time jerk a cord attached to the dummy's arm and then up went that stiff right arm to wave in clumsy benediction, bringing in reply almost invariably laughter from the passersby. Rain or shine, night and day, the wooden soldier sat on the stump and during most of the daylight hours Peter Joshman sat in his rocking chair, alert, attentive.

S. Jay, believe it or not, was amused.

"What the hell!" he said. "The old man always was a little crazy. At least it keeps him out of trouble."

The children, never surfeited, wanted more of the same. And that was something to do with his evenings, to fashion a whole family to go with the wooden soldier, a plump wife and a child, a Negro servant in a white coat, to seat some, stand the others. What a spectacle when they all waved to you at once as you were passing by! By the end of a year since the road had been opened, this curious gallery was something to look forward to, a landmark almost, almost a work of art.

There were three of them, machines, motorcycles, three drivers, keen- and hard- and brown-faced as hawks, cut like figures from old coins, trim in tight levis and glossy leather jackets that caught like sails at the breeze of their speed, and behind them the three girls, each plump-thighed, straddling the lean and agile machines, each, hair blowing like the hair of mermaids in the waves, clinging with tense hands to the wide-belted waists of the drivers. The road sang beneath them. The landscape fled, glazed, past the wind-whipped corners of their eyes. The sun dazzled off the asphalt in bright fragments like breaking glass. And the highway was theirs; they owned it, weaving among the placid and safe cars, slashing around and about them as the trout, fine as a blade, moves among the drowned shadows of swans. The road sang for them, tormented, and the conventional landscape shivered and hurtled backwards, unnoticed.

Rounding a curve the Leader came on a long straight piece

of road. It stretched towards the horizon and vanished there, empty, glistening, a holy invitation and a challenge, and, hearing his companions coming behind him, he leaned forward, crouched and opened up with a great lunge of speed. He grinned, hearing the girl squeal, hearing his friends' and rivals' engines take on the same defiant tone, accepting his dare. Nothing on either side to contend with, only the green, shocked slash pines and ahead the regular pale fields of truck farms, a few shacks, and perhaps what was a few of them bunched at one place like clod-footed dummies by the roadside. Give them something to remember, something to talk about, he was thinking, edging close to that side of the road so that he'd shower them with the noise and the dust of his passage. Nothing before or after would sweep by them so close and with such controlled violence. Let them have something to dream about. The Leader grinned to himself.

Peter Joshman was dozing. The road had been empty for quite a while. It was late in the day, not late enough for people to start returning from the beaches, but too late for the ordinary tourist to be going there. Peter dozed and listened to the bees in the garden, heard a humming in his half-dream—louder and more profound now than the vague bees, and much nearer—blinked, looked slowly, and then saw the three machines in the very instant of their passing, almost too late to wave. And with a start he jerked his rigging of cords and all the wooden arms popped up at once waving wildly as they passed. Startled, the three seemed to explode, shot away from each other, skidded, reeled, whizzed, tilted on the edge of the drainage ditches on either side, amid a clear soprano of girls' screaming, somehow righted themselves unscathed, and resumed their proper course a half-mile or so down the road, though he could see, laughing to himself, they were moving much slower now, abreast, in solemn formation going away.

When they reached the gas station at the crossroads called Evergreen, they stopped, pulled up under the shade of the roof, and dismounted. The three girls fled, rubber-jointed as drunks, to the door marked *Ladies*. The Leader leaned back, breathless, against a gas pump and spat into a rainbow smear of oil and grease by his feet.

"Jesus Christ! Did you see what I did?"

"A bunch of loonies."

"What were they trying to do, kill us?"

"Christ!" the Leader again, recovered, composed. "I thought we was all gone. Liquidated, dead."

They laughed together. Then they asked Smalley, who owned the station, what it was they had seen, and he told them about Peter Joshman and his wooden dummies.

"What is it with him?"

"What's he trying to prove?"

"I wouldn't know," Smalley said. "He sure gets a kick out of it."

"Some kick! The son of a bitch liked to have killed all of us."

"This must be the first time you boys ever come down this road."

"Yeah, but we'll know all about it coming back."

There came at twilight a summer cloudburst. For more than an hour Peter Joshman had been watching the dark clouds massing, swelling. Just as the sun went down and the whole flat countryside seemed to glow with an inner light, the rain began to fall in rich thick drops, soon pelting the dusty yard, rattling on the roof, shining on the slick road. He watched half-sadly, his forlorn wooden figures, unable to come out of the rain, standing, sitting, their weathered clothing steaming. Something would have to be done about them. Then he heard S. Jay come into the house by the back door, heavy-footed, stamping his feet, breathing hard from running across the field in the rain, and Peter stood up, stretched, and limped inside for his supper.

"Old-timer," S. Jay said, his wide young white-toothed mouth full of food, "how was your road today?"

"Is it Grandaddy's road?" one of the children asked.

"No, honey," his daughter answered for him. "The road belongs to the state."

"Be nice if it *was* your road," S. Jay said. "You could put up a tollgate out there. If you charged everybody who went by a dime, you'd be a rich man in no time. Then we could *all* sit on the front stoop and watch."

"Let's charge everybody ten cents, Grandaddy."

"You could at least charge them to look at your dummies," S. Jay said. "Maybe just ten cents a wave would be a good price."

"You-all hush picking on Daddy," his daughter said. "He loves those dummies."

"Well, that's something, anyway," S. Jay said. "It's nice to know he cares about something."

After the rain stopped it was cooler and Peter sat again on the porch, in the first dark, the first stars, watching the cars coming back. Sometimes if they happened to drive close to the shoulder of the road, their headlights suddenly picked up the group of wooden figures, bathed them in expensive light, and he in reply gave his cords a pull and blessed those night riders with a lackadaisical wave.

The three, his enemies now, though he had no way to know it, were already on the road, returning. It hadn't been the day it might have been for them. Once they had arrived at the beach, they headed south, leaving the resort town with its motels and neon gardens, its bright drugstores and bars and camera shops behind them, the rows of cottages along the dunes, troubling the dust of a narrow road which ran along just behind the dunes, past even the forlorn and separate "nigger" beach and far on to a place where at last even the road ended, came to a circle centered on a huge clump of palmetto, the road ending abruptly at a clump of green growth, higher than any dune. It was said to be an old Indian burial mound. They parked their motorcycles out of sight and climbed over the dunes to the beach.

"What did we come down here for?" one of the girls asked. Just like a girl.

"We're going swimming, ain't we?" the Leader said.

"I thought—" the girl answered. "But I didn't bring *my bathing suit*. I thought you said we could rent one."

"You know something," he said. "Neither did I."

The others laughed, but laughter did not work at all. With one of the girls reluctant, unpersuadable, the other two were forced by immemorial tribal custom to side with her, to come to her defense, and in the end the three girls sat on the dunes and smoked and chatted with each other while the three young men frolicked, half-hearted, in lean tan exhibition amid the crisp surf. There was no hope for them and, after a while, the men, feeling foolish now, dressed and started back, grim, frustrated.

When they reached the resort town again, they met by a red light.

"That son of a bitch!" the Leader said.

"Who?"

"That bastard with the dummies by the road."

So with mounting rage against the total injustice of the afternoon, the three drivers, hating the hands now that clung to their belts, hating the rich, unseen knowledge of blown hair behind them, drove back the way they had come. It had been raining and the highway was slick and thrilling. They

160

frightened their rivals in fat cars, forced them to clear the way.

Peter Joshman must have heard them coming. It was a solemn unison of buzzing sound that preceded the grim trinity of avengers as they came, slowing down as they passed through Evergreen, looking for their victims, three lights as bright and single as the Cyclops' furious eye, in formation as if passing in review. He must have heard them before he saw them and may have guessed then, for the first time, what was going to happen. Anyway, he didn't move. From aimless, really impersonal malice like that of the trench mortar that shredded and took away his leg, there was no moving, only a waiting to suffer or, by sheer luck, to be saved. He may even have closed his eyes and not seen them when they stopped and fell on the foolish wooden figures in the dark. Shouting, cursing as they stripped off clothing, they broke the wooden bodies to pieces, stamped heads into the dust.

S. Jay heard them, came out of his bedroom in his under-shorts roaring, across the porch in one long-legged leap, his shotgun bursting forth, both barrels at once, an orange choleric mushroom against the astounded night sky, hitting nothing, or nothing important (one of the girls squealed like a frightened pig, but maybe it was nothing more than the noise and the shock of heavy birdshot in the air). He ran towards them then, as they clambered on their motorcycles, stamped furiously on starters, cursing them as they fled down the road, knelt to reload, kneeling among the shattered corpses of the figures and the debris, the stuffing, glass eyes and torn clothing, but he was too late. Still in a rage, S. Jay fired again high and pointlessly into the trees, and the leaves sighed. He came back to the house slowly, dragging his gun-butt in the dust.

"Son of a bitches!" he said. "Old-timer, they wrecked all your dummies."

"Maybe it's just as well."

"What do you mean, *just as well?*" S. Jay yelled at him. "It's my land, ain't it? I'll kill the son of a bitches if they come back."

"I say maybe it's just as well," Peter said. "It was a crazy idea in the first place. I let it get a hold to me and started to care too much. Nothing is worth caring much about. Nothing."

"I can't figure you out for the life of me," S. Jay said. "Ain't you going to try and fix them up again?"

"I don't know," Peter Joshman said. "I'll sleep on it. It takes me a while to get used to things."

an evening performance

For several weeks, maybe a month or so, there she stood, a plump woman in a sequined one-piece bathing suit, poised on a stylized tower which rose into the very clouds, like Jacob's dreamy ladder, with here and there around it a few birds in tense swift V's, and below, far, far below, there was a tub, flaming and terrible, into which she was surely going to plunge. Beneath in fiery letters was printed: ONE OF THE FABULOUS WONDERS OF MODERN TIMES / STELLA THE HIGH DIVER / SHE DIVES ONE HUNDRED FEET / INTO A FLAMING CAULDRON.

These posters had appeared mysteriously one Monday morning, and they were everywhere, on store windows, on the sides of buildings, on telephone and light poles, tacked to green trees; and you can believe they caused a stir. The children on the way to school (for it was just the beginning of the school year) bunched around them in excited clusters —staring at her buxom magnificence, wondering at her daring—and buzzed about it all day long like a hive of disturbed bees. By midmorning grumbling adults were ripping the posters down from windows and buildings, and a couple of policemen went up and down the main street and some of the side streets, taking them off telephone and light poles. But there were so many! And it was such a mystery. Lurid and unsettling as a blast of trumpets, they had come nevertheless in the night as silently as snow.

It would be later, much later, that the night counterman at the Paradise Diner on the outskirts of town, beyond the last glare of filling stations and the winking motels and the brilliant inanity of used-car lots—where, no matter how carnival-colorful with flags and whirligigs, no matter how brightly lit, the rows of cars stood like sad wooden horses from some carousel set out to graze—it would be later when he would remember that the man, the angry little man with the limp, had stopped there for coffee that same night that the posters had appeared.

In spite of all effort, a few of the posters remained, tantalizing in their vague promise of a future marvel, teased by the wind and the weather, faded by the still summer-savage sun and the first needling rains of autumn, the red letters blurring and dribbling away, fuzzy now as if they had been written by a shaking finger in something perishable like blood. Talked about for a while—and there were those who swore they remembered seeing such a thing and certainly those who had *heard* of it, a subject of some debate and even a little sermonizing in certain of the more fundamentalist churches where amusement is, by definition, nearly equiva-

164

lent to vice—the promise faded with the posters. There were few who hoped that Stella would ever dive there, fewer still who believed in her coming. It seemed, after all, only another joke of some kind, pointless, mirthless, and in a strange way deeply distressing.

Then one evening in late October with the weather now as cool and gray as wash water the truck came and parked in the field by the old Fairgrounds. At first it was nothing to take much notice of, merely a big, battered truck and pretty soon an Army surplus squad tent, sprouting (sagging in a most unmilitary, careless way) like a khaki mushroom beside it.

And there were people.

There were three of them. There was the man, gimpy (his left leg *might* have been wooden), his face puckered and fierce and jowly and quizzical like a Boston bulldog, his eyes glazed and almost lightless like the little button eyes of a doll; fierce and tired he seemed, spoke in mutters, showing from time to time a ruined mouth with teeth all awry and at all angles like an old fence; and sometimes around the town, shopping for groceries at the Supermarket, once taking a load of dirty clothes to the Wishywashy, buying cigarettes and aspirins and comic books at the drugstore, and busily sorting out bolts and nuts and screws and clamps and brackets at the hardware store (for what?), he talked to himself, a harsh, steady, and indecipherable monotone. There was the little girl, a frail thing made entirely of glazed china with altogether unlikely eyes and hair as bright as new pennies, like a shower of money, richly brushed and shining and worn long to her waist. She wore white always, starched and ironed and fabulously clean; and the woman had to wonder how her mother (?)—the woman anyhow—living in a sagging tent and a worn-out truck, managed that. The little girl was heard to answer to the name of Angel and did not play with the other children who sometimes, after school, gathered in shrill clots around the tent and the truck to stare until the terrible man came out, limping, waving a pick handle, and chased them away.

The woman was an equal curiosity. She was short, broad-shouldered, wide-hipped, huge-handed, sturdy as a man. Her hair, dyed redder than you'd care to believe, was cut in a short bowl. She appeared to be in early middle age, though she might easily have been old—she wore such savage make-up, wild, accented, slanted eyes, a mouth of flame, and always two perfectly round spots of red like dying roses on her high cheekbones. Still, she had a smile that was a glory and she smiled often. She was not heard to speak to anyone and when she was talked to she smiled and stared, uncomprehending. It was not long before everyone knew she was a mute; it was proved when she was seen to communicate with the man, her hands as swift as wings and not a word.

The truth came out like a jack-in-the-box in a week or so. One fine morning the man had unloaded an enormous pile of boards and pipes beside the truck, and by noon he had erected in the center of the field what seemed to be the beginnings of a good-size drilling derrick.

"For oil?" That was the joke around town before a few of the prominent men and a policeman went out there in cars, parked at the edge of the field, and walked to where he was working. He paid them no mind at all as they straggled towards him, and, as they drew near, they could see that he was sweat-soaked and working at his task with an unbecoming fury, all in hasty, jerky gestures like a comedian in a silent movie. He did not stop his work until they spoke to him.

"What are you trying to do here?" the policeman said.

The man spat and put his heavy wrench on the ground.

"What the hell does it look like I'm doing?" he said and someone giggled. "I'm putting up the tower."

"What kind of a tower?"

"The tower for Stella," the man said, sighing between his teeth. "How can she dive without a tower? That's logic, aint' it?"

"Oh," the policeman said. "You got to have a license to put on any kind of a exhibition around here."

The lame man lowered his head, seemed to shrink and sag like a slowly deflating balloon, and muttered to himself. Finally he raised his head and looked at them, and they could see the tears glisten in his eyes.

"How much do the license cost?" he said.

"Twenty-five dollars."

"We don't have to do the dive," the man said. "We got a lots of tricks. I can put up just a little bit of a trapeze and Angel can do things that would make your eyes pop out of your head. If worse comes to worse we don't have to build nothing at all. If I have to I can stand on the back end of the truck and swallow swords and fire and Angel and Stella can dance."

"Any kind of exhibition costs twenty-five dollars for the license."

The man shrugged and hung his head again.

"Don't you have the money?"

He shook his head, but still would not look at them.

"Well, what the hell?" the policeman said. "You better take that tower down and get on out of town. We got a law—"

"Wait a minute," a merchant said. "You aim to sell tickets, don't you?"

The man nodded.

"If you put on the high dive, I reckon you may get as many as a thousand to see it, counting kids and all. What kind of a price do you charge?"

When the man looked up again, he had his ruined smile for them all. "Two-bits a head," he said. "We got a roll of tickets printed up and everything."

The merchant made a hasty calculation. "All right," he said. "I'll tell you what I'll do. I'll get your license for you and you cut me in for half of what you take."

"*Half?*" the man said. "Half is too much. That's a dirty shame. It ain't hardly worth it for half. Besides, the high dive is dangerous."

"Take it or leave it."

"All right," the man said. "I can't do nothing but take it."

"Tell you what else I'll do," the merchant said. "I got a nigger boy helps me down to the store. I'll send him to help you put that tower up. How soon can you put on the show?"

"Tomorrow evening if the weather's good."

While they were standing there talking the woman had come across the field from the tent and stood holding the hand of the little girl, smiling her wonderful smile. She seemed to have not the least notion of what was going on, but as they walked away they saw that she had turned on the man, unsmiling, and as he shook and shook his head, her hands flashed at him like the wings of a wild bird in a cage.

All that day the tower grew and by noon of the next day it was finished. It stood not nearly so tall as the cloud- and bird-troubled structures on the posters, but menacingly high, a rickety skeleton that swayed a little in the light breeze. All the way to the top there was rope ladder and on the top a small platform with an extended plank for a diving board. At the foot of the tower the lame man had created a large wooden and canvas tank into which he and the woman and the Negro who worked for the merchant poured buckets of water, drawn from a public spigot, all afternoon, until it was filled about to the depth of a tall man. There was a large GI can of gasoline nearby. The lame man rigged up a string of colored lights and two large searchlights intended to focus on the diver at the top. He set up a card table at the corner where the main road turned into the Fairgrounds. He put up a few of the posters on the poles and the side of the truck, and by midafternoon everything was ready.

Then the weather turned. The wind came from the north, steady, and with it a thin rain like cold needles. The tower moved with the wind and shone with wet. The woman and the little girl stayed in the tent. The lame man stood at the card table, with a newspaper on his head to keep off the rain, waiting for the first customers to arrive.

Just at dark the merchant arrived. There was a good crowd, equal at least to their expectations, gathered in a ring around the tower, standing in raincoats and underneath umbrellas, silently waiting.

"Well," the merchant said, "it looks like we did all right irregardless of the weather."

"Yeah," the man replied. "Except she don't want to do it."

"What's that?"

"I mean it's too risky at a time like this."

"You should have thought of that before," the merchant said. "If you don't go through with it now, no telling *what* might happen."

"Oh, we'll give them a show," the man said. "I'll swallow swords if I have to. We'll do something."

"She's got to dive," the merchant said. "Or else you got a case of fraud on your hands."

After that the two of them went into the tent. Inside the

woman was sitting on an Army cot, wrapped up in a man's bathrobe, and the little girl was beside her. It was cold and damp and foul in the tent. The merchant winced at the smell of it.

"Tell her she's got to do it."

The lame man waved his hands in deft code to her. She moved her hands slowly in reply and, smiling, shook her head. Outside the people had started to clap their hands in unison.

"She says it's too dangerous. It's dangerous anyhow, but on a night like this—"

"Come on," the merchant said. "It can't be that bad. There must be a trick to it."

The lame man shook his head.

"No, sir," he said. "It ain't no trick to it. It's the most dangerous activity in the world. She don't like to do it one bit."

"That's a fine thing," the merchant said. "Just fine and dandy. If she don't like it, why the hell do you put up posters and build towers and sell tickets, that's what I'd like to know."

"Somebody's got to do it. If it wasn't us, it would just have to be somebody else."

"Oh my God!" the merchant said, throwing up his hands. "Now you listen here. If you don't get the show going in five minutes, I'll have you all slapped right in the jail. Five minutes."

He opened the flap of the tent and went out into the dark and the chill rain. He could hear the little girl crying and the lame man muttering to himself.

Almost at once the lame man followed him. He started up the truck and turned on all the lights. Then the woman appeared in her outsize bathrobe and wearing now a white bathing cap. She walked to the foot of the tower and leaned against it, one hand clutching a rung of the rope ladder, smiling.

"Ladies and gentlemen," the lame man said. "You are about to witness a performance that defies the laws of nature and science. This little lady you see before you is fixing to climb to the top of the tower. There, at that terrible altitude, she's going to stand and dive into a flaming tank of water that's barely six feet deep. You won't believe your eyes. It's a marvel of the modern world. How does she do it? Some of you will ask. Now some show people will give you all kinds of fancy reasons for how and why they do their work. They'll tell you they learned it from the wise men of the East. They'll tell you about magicians and dreams and the Secrets of The Ancient World. Not us. The way that Stella does this dive is skill, skill pure and simple. When Stella climbs that tower and dives into the flames she's doing something anyone could do who has the heart and the skill and the nerve for it. That's what's different and special about our show. When Stella sails through the air and falls in the fire and comes up safe and smiling, she is the living and breathing proof of the boundless possibility of all mankind. It should make you happy. It should make you glad to be alive."

"Let's get on with it," someone shouted, and the crowd hollered and whistled.

"All right, we won't give you no special build-up," the lame man continued in an even voice. "We just say, there it is. See for yourself. And without further ado I give you Stella, the high diver."

He touched her. She removed the bathrobe and opening her arms wide, showed herself, pale and stocky in the tight bathing suit with the winking sequins. Then she turned and began to climb the rope ladder. It was a perilous ascent and the ladder swung with the weight of her. When she reached the top, she rested, kneeling on the platform; then she stood up and unhitched the rope ladder and it fell away in a limp curve like a dead snake.

The crowd gasped.

"Do you see?" the lame man shouted. "Now there's no other way to get down except by diving!"

He hobbled over to the tank and sloshed gasoline on top of the water. He stood back and looked up at her. She stood on the diving plank and looked down. The tower rattled and moved in the wind and she seemed very small and far away. She stood on the end of the plank looking down, then she signalled to the man. He lit the gasoline and jumped back awkwardly as the flames shot up. Just at that instant she dived. Soaring and graceful, her arms wide apart, she seemed for a breathless time to hang at that great height in the wind, caught in the brilliant snare of the searchlights. Then she seemed to fold into herself like a fan and straight and swift as a thrown spear she descended, plummeting into the tank with a great and sparkling flash of fire and water.

There was a hushed moment while the crowd waited to see if she was still alive, but she emerged, climbed out of the tank smiling, and showed herself to them, damp and unscathed. She put on her bathrobe and hurried back to the tent. Some of the people began to leave, but many stood gazing at the tower and the vacant tank. The lame man switched off the lights and followed after her, disappearing into the tent.

The merchant entered the tent. The three of them, sitting in a row along the edge of the cot, were eating something out of a can. A red lantern glared at their feet.

"Is that all?" the merchant said. "I mean is that all there is to it?"

The man nodded.

"Kind of brief, don't you think, for two-bits a head?"

"That's all there is to it," the man said. "She could have killed herself. Ain't that enough for one evening? They ought to be glad."

The merchant looked at her. She was eating from the can and seemed as happy as could be.

"Can't you swallow some swords or something? We want everybody to feel they got their money's worth."

"Godamnit, they did!" the lame man said. "They got all they're going to."

The merchant tried to persuade him to do something more, but he continued to refuse. So the merchant took his share of the money and left them. Soon the rest of the people left too.

The next morning the three of them were gone. The tower was gone, the truck, the tent, and they might never have been there at all, for all the trace they left. Except for the dark spots on the grass where the flaming water had splashed, except for a few posters remaining (and they were not true to fact or life), there was no trace of them.

But if the evening performance had been brief, it remained with them, haunting, a long time afterwards. Some of the preachers continued to denounce it as the work of the devil himself. The drunkards and tellers of tall tales embroidered on it and exaggerated it and preserved it until the legend of that high dive was like a beautiful tapestry before which they might act out their lives, strangely dwarfed and shamed. The children pestered and fidgeted and wanted to know when the three would come again.

A wise man, a cripple himself, said it had been a terrible thing.

"It made us all sophisticated," he said. "We can't be pleased by any ordinary marvels any more—tightrope walkers, fire-eaters, pretty girls being fired out of cannons. It's going to take a regular apocalypse to make us raise our eyebrows again."

He was almost right, as nearly correct as a wise man could hope to be. How could he even imagine that more than one aging, loveless woman slept better ever after, smiled as she dreamed herself gloriously descending for all the world to see from a topless tower into a lake of flame?

in the BRIAR patch

a book of stories

BY GEORGE GARRETT

was composed in ten-point Caledonia, three
points leaded, with display in Libra, and printed
by letterpress on 60 pound Warren's Olde Style,
laid finish, made by the S. D. Warren Company.
Design and decorations were done by Jo Alys
Downs. The book was manufactured by the
Printing Division of the University of Texas.